THE LOST GIRL'S MIRACLE

The Victorian Love Sagas
Book 3

Annie Brown

The Lost Girl's Miracle — Annie Brown

Copyright © 2024 Annie Brown

The right of Annie Brown identified as the author of this work, has been asserted in accordance with the Copyright Designs and Patents Act 1988.

All rights reserved. No part of this work may be reproduced in any material form (including photocopying or storing by any electronic means and whether or not transiently or incidentally to some other use of this publication) without write permission of the copyright holder except in accordance with the provisions of the Copyright, Designs and Patents Act 1988.

Applications for the copyright holder's permission to reproduce any part of this publication should be addressed to the publishers.

Contents

1. Chapter 1   1
2. Chapter 2   8
3. Chapter 3   11
4. Chapter 4   14
5. Chapter 5   17
6. Chapter 6   24
7. Chapter 7   27
8. Chapter 8   31
9. Chapter 9   34
10. Chapter 10   37
11. Chapter 11   41
12. Chapter 12   47
13. Chapter 13   52
14. Chapter 14   56

15.	Chapter 15	61
16.	Chapter 16	67
17.	Chapter 17	73
18.	Chapter 18	79
19.	Chapter 19	84
20.	Chapter 20	89
21.	Chapter 21	92
22.	Chapter 22	95
23.	Chapter 23	99
24.	Chapter 24	102
25.	Chapter 25	107
26.	Chapter 26	110
27.	Chapter 27	115
28.	Chapter 28	119
29.	Chapter 29	122
30.	Chapter 30	126
31.	Chapter 31	129
32.	Chapter 32	133
33.	Chapter 33	136
34.	Chapter 34	141
35.	Chapter 35	144
36.	Chapter 36	149
37.	Chapter 37	156
38.	Chapter 38	159

39.	Chapter 39	162
40.	Chapter 40	165
41.	Chapter 41	170
42.	Chapter 42	174
43.	Chapter 43	178
44.	Chapter 44	181
45.	Chapter 45	185
46.	Chapter 46	187
47.	Chapter 47	192
48.	Chapter 48	195
Epilogue		198
About the author		203

Chapter One

"Pa, pa, did you have a good day at work today?" Alice eagerly greeted the person she was closest to in life, rushing over to him as he entered through the door. His apron was still around his neck and his hands were black from extracting paraffin from the oil to make his candles, the side of his thumbs were dry with blood.

"Seeing you, Alice, has made it even better," he said, lifting his daughter and spinning her around. The house echoed with laughter as Edward smiled, watching his daughter's joy from such a simple thing. "Now then, where's your ma?"

Edward walked over to Katherine and put his arms around her waist whilst she was standing facing the stove. "Hello, my love, mmm, something smells good," he said, trying to nuzzle into her neck.

"Edward, please, I'm busy," Katherine said with impatience that made Edward move his hands and step back. Katherine turned around to see the disappointment on her husband's face. "I'm sorry; it's just been a long day. Our new foreman, who started a couple of months ago, somehow manages to make us work even harder," she said, exhaustion evident on her face.

"I'm sorry," said Edward sympathetically, "the candles are just not selling well at the moment. I'm not sure if people are going into the city to buy them or are using gas lamps instead. I suppose they are a small luxury. Either way, something will have to change, we can't have you getting tired all the time. It must be hard working there, and you have to keep an eye on Peter and Alice, too. Is this new foreman as harsh on them as he is on the others?"

Katherine shook her head and continued stirring yesterday's old vegetables swirling around in the murky, cloudy broth. They had seen better days.

Edward and Katherine had been married ten years and had lived in Willowbrook all their lives. From the day they were born to courting and walking in the hay fields as the sun went down and starting a family, it was home. It was comfortable, safe, and no matter how hard times got, they could return and hold each other tight. It was perfect for them.

Katherine worked at the nail mill, and Edward continued trying to make money from his candle making. Meanwhile, eight-year-old Alice and twelve-year-old Peter had been forced to work in the mill too. Times were hard and disconcerting, so any extra money they could get their hands on was welcomed. Life was hard, but it was set to get a whole lot worse.

Katherine lifted the pot of broth to the table where a loaf of bread was already taking centre stage. Alice had sat down at the table ready for her dinner. She was exhausted and rested her head in her hands. "Alice, wake up, Alice!"

Peter looked on, just as tired, his head nodding so sharply and hard, Edward feared it coming away from him and rolling onto the table.

"Come on, my little stars, at least eat something before you fall asleep, or you will wake up hungry, and we can't have that, can we? You have work again tomorrow."

Edward sat next to his children, put his arms around them, and pulled them close.

"Don't do that, Edward; we are about to eat dinner!"

Edward looked at Katherine and knew something was wrong. She was exhausted from the long, hard labour, but she wasn't usually as tetchy as this. Maybe he would speak to her about it later.

Just as they were about to take a mouthful, there was a loud knock at the door. Edward stood up after looking at his wife, sighed, and made his way over to the door to open it. He rolled his eyes at the sight of the short, stumpy man standing in front of him, buttons bursting at the seams.

"Now then, Edward, you know your rent is due. Don't be asking me for more time like you did last month, or I may be adding interest," Charles Bellingham was a plump character with bright red, rosy cheeks, a checked waistcoat, and a suit that looked as if it had seen better days. His shoes were well polished though, and he held his stubby hands across his belly to make him look as if he had some authority over the candlemaker and his wife.

"Time sure does come round quick, Mr Bellingham. How are you today? Are you having a good day?"

"I will be even better when you stop playing for time and hand your rent over."

"Here!" Katherine said, approaching her husband from behind and handing over the coins. "I think you will find it's all there, thank you," Katherine said, glancing at her husband from the side as she went back into the house.

"Got your wife looking after you now, have you, Edward? Can't afford to keep your family going by yourself?"

Edward's neck flushed pink. "Thank you, Mr Bellingham, that will be all, my food is going cold." Edward turned around and kicked the door shut behind him with a loud thud and breathed a sigh of relief.

"And I'll have none of that attitude either, Edward, or it goes up, do you hear me? It goes up!" Mr Bellingham shouted and thumped his fist on the window before stomping off.

Edward walked back to the table and sat down quietly. He looked at Katherine, feeling ashamed he wasn't providing for the family. He picked up his spoon, lifted it to his mouth, but then dropped it in his food and pushed his bowl away.

"Come on, Edward, eat up, you will be hungry after a long day." Katherine neither had the inclination nor desire to talk about Edward not making enough money. She had a long day with another one tomorrow and another six after that. Initially, when Katherine found work at the nail mill, she was looking forward to it, a chance for her to step out on her own. She had married young, and all she had known was a life with Edward. She loved him with all her heart and adored Peter and Grace, but recently, she had been feeling frustrated with him, feeling as if all the responsibility was on her to pay the bills and the rent. And now, with Peter starting at the factory, she wanted to keep an eye on her son while he was working.

"I've lost my appetite."

"Don't be like that, I've made it especially."

"No, you haven't. You've cobbled together some wrinkly veg, boiled some water, and hoped it would stem all our appetites. But the truth is we're all starving, I can't provide for my family, and you are paying the rent."

Katherine looked at her husband nonchalantly. She desperately wanted orders at his workshop to pick up so they could at least afford pigs' trotters and a jug of milk when needed.

"We are in this together, Edward, we get through this together, do you hear me?" She stood up and cleared the bowls from the table, not one had been licked clean. She slammed the dishes down and held on to the table. The worn-out young wife and mother gazed down at the grains of wood hoping they would take her mind away from the harsh reality of life as it was today.

It wasn't frustration though that was worrying Katherine; it was Frank, the foreman, who had been working at the mill for almost two months. He seemed to have taken a shine to Katherine. She kept herself to herself and just got on with her work, however, Frank had other ideas and had ended up in one of the storerooms with her on more than one occasion. Katherine could never escape and felt she had to keep her mouth shut for fear of being dismissed. She couldn't afford to get sacked and would struggle to find work elsewhere. The nail mill was the biggest employer in town, and Frank knew it. He took advantage of Katherine and knew how she felt, so he did it even more.

Katherine was tired and worried where it would lead. Frank had shown no signs of bothering the other females, and he knew that Katherine was married, but it didn't seem to stop him.

"Right then, Alice, let's get you to bed before you fall asleep completely, you're far too old to be carried to bed these days." Edward took his daughter, the youngest of his two children, and led her upstairs. "I'll take her up, love; you go and sit by the fire," he said looking at Katherine. The ice-cold atmosphere warmed with every passing minute.

"I love you, pa," Alice said as she shuffled further down the bed under her blankets.

"I love you too, Alice, always. Now get yourself off to sleep, you have to be up early in the morning to go to the mill."

"I hope that horrible man isn't there again, he's not very nice to us."

"What do you mean, horrible man, Alice? Has someone upset you?"

"No, pa, it's just that he's not very nice to ma."

Edward blinked slowly and sighed, it appeared Katherine wasn't telling him the whole truth and he feared it was more serious than she was letting on. "Go to sleep, and I will go and check your ma is okay." Before he left the room, his daughter's eyes were closed and her body twitched as she drifted into much needed unconsciousness.

Edward crept down the stairs, his hand running down the banister. He walked over to his wife and set his tall, muscular frame down into the threadbare armchair opposite her by the fire. "How are you, my love? I mean how are you, really? Are you hiding something from me? You look like you've had a terrible day. I didn't want to say as much in front of the children."

Peter looked over at his parents but didn't say a word.

"Oh, I'm fine, Edward. It's just heavy work, that's all, and it's the anniversary of George's death this week, did you remember?"

Edward hung his head down in shame. He remembered his young son fondly but had forgotten the anniversary with everything else on his mind. He didn't have to say anything, Katherine knew but didn't want to add to her husband's guilt, she could tell he was already feeling fragile.

"I thought I would go and visit his grave; would you like to come?"

"Yes, of course I will come. Alice and Peter as well, okay? The four of us can go and say a prayer for him."

Katherine had a tear in her eye. "I don't think I will ever forget him, Edward, not ever. Every day just seems hard without him, and I thought I should have done more to save him. I dread every day that Alice and Peter will catch it too, then we will be bereft of our beloved children."

"I'll be okay, ma, don't worry about me," Peter said.

"He's right, you know. That will never happen," Edward said as he got up from his chair and knelt in front of his wife, taking her hand. "They are both safe and always will be, I promise."

"I hope so, Edward; I really do."

"And what about this horrible man at work? Is he bothering you, too?"

"Horrible man? What are you talking about," Katherine said, dismissing his question and wanting to move away from her husband.

"Alice told me, she said she hoped the horrible man wouldn't be there tomorrow."

"Oh, take no notice. She's only young and doesn't know what she's talking about. The foreman is strict, but he has to be, doesn't he, to make sure the work gets done?"

"As long as he isn't bothering you, Katherine."

"No, not at all; it's nothing," she said as she stood up and walked over to the stove, wanting to put aside the whole subject.

Peter blinked and looked at his pa before giving him a considered look.

Chapter Two

The following morning, the fog lay heavily over the cobbled streets of Willowbrook as if reluctant to reveal the secrets hidden within. The nail mill loomed ahead, its imposing structure casting long shadows over the labouring souls who entered its gates each day. Among them were Alice and Peter, the weight of their family's struggles resting heavily on their young shoulders.

As they entered the bustling mill, Katherine's gaze met the wary eyes of her children. Alice's youthful innocence was obvious against the harsh reality of the factory, and Peter, at twelve, carried a burden beyond his years.

Katherine knelt beside them, offering whispered reassurances. "Be strong, my darlings. Remember, we are here together." With determined nods, they ventured forth, embarking on another gruelling day's work.

Alice tried her best to keep an eye on her older brother, though she couldn't shake the feeling that something ominous lurked within the mill's walls.

As the children and their mother entered the mill, Alice flinched at every sound, sending her stomach into knots and making her eyes scout around the building before she took another step. Peter chose to ignore the weary faces at the machines and the cries for help, as a machine trapped yet another finger in the harsh reality of what was workhouse life.

As the day wore on, Katherine's thoughts kept returning to Frank, the foreman whose unwanted advances had made her life at the mill increasingly unbearable. She had hoped that today would be different, that he would leave her be, but her optimism proved futile. Frank's watchful eye followed her, and at the slightest opportunity, he cornered her once more, his words laced with malice.

"Mrs Hartman," he sneered, his voice dripping with false courtesy. The sweaty foreman took a step closer to the worker.

It made Katherine feel sick to the stomach and shiver inside. But she couldn't do anything. If the young mother once put up a fuss or told anyone what the skin-crawling foreman was up to, her family would be out on the streets. Katherine swore she heard his tongue licking his lips as he spoke.

"I couldn't help but notice your delicate beauty among these rough workers. Perhaps we should find a moment to chat privately," he whispered into her delicate ear.

Katherine, her heart pounding, tried to evade his advances. "Mr Wilson, there's work to be done. I cannot afford to be idle; you'll dock my wages and we desperately need the money."

His sharp laughter echoed in the dimly lit room. "Idle, Mrs Hartman? No, I think not. I wouldn't say you're idle, far from it. In fact, I promise I will never use that word again as far as you're concerned."

Unable to escape, Katherine felt a growing sense of despair. Her mind raced, considering the consequences of reporting Frank's harassment. It was a precarious situation. Her job at the nail mill was her family's lifeline whilst orders for candles were slow and low at her husband's workshop, and she dared not jeopardise it.

Each day, she bore the weight of this dark secret alone, unable to share her torment with Edward. "Please, Mr Wilson, just let me get on with my work."

"My patience is wearing thin, my office now. Unless you want punishment." The vile foreman licked his lips and looked down at her.

Katherine begrudgingly followed Frank Wilson to his office. Her hands were sweaty, and she blinked slowly knowing what was to come.

Chapter Three

Edward toiled tirelessly in his candle-making shop, striving to improve the future of the small workshop based behind the house. Even though light was a necessity, the workshop had few visitors. Instead, people would make do with oil lamps and the last light of the day rather than spend their pennies on what was seen as a luxury. And on the rare occasion where the wealthy would place an order, it wasn't enough to cover everything. The dwindling demand for candles weighed heavily on him, and he couldn't help but feel a growing sense of inadequacy as the bills piled up. The memory of his promise to Katherine, to shield their family from hardship, drove him forward. But he couldn't help but think his wife was in trouble.

As his dark thoughts rattled around in his head, a stranger entered the workshop ringing the bell above the door. The chime shook Edward from his thoughts, and he looked up. "Hello, can I help?" The stranger dressed in a dark suit, made Edward feel envious.

Edward's eyes scanned the stranger up and down waiting for a response to his greeting. "I, erm—I've not seen you in here before, are you looking for anything in particular?" Edward felt a quiver of anxiety at his core anticipating a big order from the finely dressed man standing in front of him. Only the upper-class would buy from him, so little wonder the visitor brought a smile to his face. *Maybe this will take the pressure off Katherine short term, do everything you can to please him.*

"We don't have Tallow candles, if that's what you're looking for, I gave them up a long time ago. Just beeswax now, they don't stink and will last longer." Edward coughed, "Sorry, sir, smell, not stink." He brought a fist to his mouth and coughed slightly again, hoping his common, dour language would go unnoticed.

"I'm looking for a big order, I trust you will be able to fulfil, I've heard good things about you."

Edward didn't know what to do with himself. He felt like he was dancing on the spot, and his hands and arms waved enthusiastically in the air, trying to show what sizes were available and at what cost.

Despite never having seen the gentleman before, he aimed to please. "Certainly, I can make any quantity, within reason of course as there is just myself. But quality and a long burn time is guaranteed. So, what do you say?"

"Excellent. Now I know I can get what I need, I'll just have one more look around and come back tomorrow."

"Can't I persuade you to order this evening, sir? I could give you a small discount if you do."

"Discount?" The gentleman looked shocked. "I'm not the type who needs a discount. Tomorrow will be just fine."

Edward gritted his teeth and breathed in through his nose, worrying that he had said too much and put his new customer off. The customer took one last look around, then tipped his hat at Edward and left without saying another word.

Edward jumped in the air when he saw the door close. *Yes, this is just the news Katherine is waiting to hear. A big order will be just what we need.*

Frank Wilson walked down the street having visited Edward's workshop and now knowing exactly what he was up against to get what he wanted.

Chapter Four

Katherine turned around from the stove to see her husband walk through the door. She gave him a weary smile, then turned back around again and continued to stir the measly broth. "It won't be long, I'm sure you're hungry." Her stomach rumbled at the sight and smell of the hot liquid on the stove. Edward walked up to his wife and put his loving arms around her waist. He nuzzled his nose and mouth into the side of her neck and felt her soft tender skin.

Katherine flinched without realising and then brushed her husband away. "I'm sorry, I just need to get this finished otherwise supper will be late."

"I'm sure it can wait while we get close."

"Please, Edward," Katherine stepped to the side. "I've had a long, tiresome day and I'm starving." She looked around briefly. "What are you so happy about, anyway? Do you have something to tell me?"

"It's nothing, I'm sure it can wait," he responded despondently.

Edward felt like his wife had reached inside and grabbed at his heart and the good feeling he had from the order coming in tomorrow. He had jovially walked home and couldn't wait to give her the good news. Now he felt deflated and that maybe the news was insignificant compared to what was going on at the mill.

As the two children finished their supper and left their parents at the table, Katherine took a deep breath. "Edward, can I talk to you about something?"

"Of course, what is it?" he asked whilst taking a slurp of the hot broth onto his tongue. He didn't look up.

"I've been thinking, perhaps it's time you got a paid job. Candles seem insufficient to provide for our family. I mean, I know I am helping as well, it's just that—well, some days I'm so exhausted I'm not sure how long I can continue at the mill. I didn't intend on staying forever, but with each day that goes by, we are relying more and more on my meagre, useless wages."

He took a deep breath in to calm the excitement and nerves, he couldn't hold his news back any longer. "The thing is, I wanted to tell you this when I got home."

Katherine blinked slowly knowing that she had brushed his advances aside. "What is it?"

"I had a visit from a well-dressed gentleman today. He is coming back tomorrow with a large order. He seems very well to do and didn't even want a discount." Edward reached his hand across the table to take his wife's. "Don't you see, Katherine, this order could see us good for months, if not years if I keep him happy." He stroked her soft skin and looked at her lovingly. He desperately wanted her away from the mill, he could see it was destroying her.

Katherine's eyes welled up with glimmers of the clear tears highlighting the red rims on the bottom of her tired eyes. "That's wonderful. How many is he buying?"

"I'm not sure, but he said he will definitely return tomorrow."

Katherine's heart sank, and she pulled her hand away. "Edward, please don't get your hopes up. We have been here before with promises of big orders from the wealthy few, only to be let down at the last minute."

Edward stood up and pushed his chair back. "Thanks for nothing. I thought you would have been pleased, but all you can do is criticise me, do you realise I'm doing my best? Do you know how it breaks my heart everyday watching you and the children going to work in that place?"

"I'm sorry, Edward. I just didn't want you to be disappointed. I love you with all of my heart. It would pain me to see you come home full of worry and regret tomorrow when he doesn't show up." Her mouth twisted a little into a smile, her weariness etched across her features. "Look, Edward, we must adapt to survive. We've faced hardships before, and we'll overcome this as well."

Edward nodded slowly. "I know. I just feel helpless." He sloped away from the kitchen shaking his head without saying another word and leaving his wife wondering if they would make it through the next few months.

She didn't want to burden him with any more troubles, so the hardship and torment she was facing at the mill would have to stay secret for now.

Chapter Five

⚘

"Come on, Alice, Peter, hurry up!" Katherine said, gripping her children's hands firmly, urging them to walk faster. "We have to be on time today, we simply can't afford to be late again."

Alice and Peter looked glum and begrudgingly quickened their pace, understanding the urgency in their mother's voice.

As they walked along the road towards the mill, Katherine felt the children's reluctance. She smiled at strangers and neighbours hoping they would just walk on by and not stop to blether. She looked down at Alice and Peter. "Watch where you are going, Alice. You slipping and falling is the last thing I need. Walk properly." She shrugged their hands hoping to speed them up.

"Ma, you're hurting me, please let go." Alice's eyes started to water at the pressure of her ma's handgrip. Katherine picked up her speed, dragging her children behind.

"Ma, I think you're hurting Alice."

Without warning, Alice screamed as she fell to the floor, tripping over her own feet, her legs ending up in a tangled mess on the wet ground. The young girl sat crying and looked up at her ma as the foggy, bleak drizzle continued to soak her bedraggled hair and pale skin.

Katherine looked at her daughter and crouched down. "Alice, please get up."

"Ma, I said you were hurting her, she was walking as fast as she could."

"Don't you dare talk to me like that, Peter, keep your nose out."

"No! You are being horrible to us, and we don't know why. It's not nice." Peter's raised voice made her stop and take a deep breath in.

"You walked so fast, ma, I couldn't keep up." Alice's tiny, calloused hands wiped the tears away from her mottled cheeks.

Katherine looked at Peter with wide eyes and then her daughter. She crouched down next to her. "Oh, Alice, I'm so sorry. I just want to avoid giving that terrible man any opportunity to reprimand us. Do you understand?"

"What does that mean, ma?"

"Shout, Alice. It means telling someone off because they are naughty."

Alice gave an understanding nod.

"Good girl, now let me help you up." Katherine reached out with both her hands and pulled her daughter to her feet.

Katherine's chest felt heavy, her breathing became restless. She didn't want to give Frank any reason to approach her, especially not after the previous encounters that had left her feeling violated and tormented, but she knew they were now running late after Alice's tumble. She shuddered at the thought of going to work, secretly wishing for an accident that would keep her away, but she knew the harsh reality - they couldn't survive without her wages, and certainly not on the meagre earnings from Edward's candle-making venture.

As they neared the mill, the clamour of the machines and the acrid smell of smouldering metal grew stronger. Katherine's anxiety gnawed at her, but she forced herself to suppress it. They entered through the back entrance, and she whispered, "Right, Alice, Peter, you know where to go. Be good, do your work, and I'll see you later."

They joined the other children, their tasks being to clean between and around the machines. As they knelt down to begin, Frank appeared behind them.

"Speed up, you two, you're late and there's plenty to be done," his voice menacing.

"Yes, sir," they replied together, turning to look into the foreman's dark and intimidating eyes.

"Don't answer me, just do it!" Frank snapped before striding away.

Meanwhile, Katherine faced Frank's unwelcome advances as he confronted her about being two minutes late. His threat of docking her pay hung heavily in the air, and Katherine knew she would have to meet him in his office at midday. "I'm sorry, sir," Katherine stammered, "I didn't realise I was late. Alice wasn't feeling too good this morning, so it took her a while to walk here. I even asked her to hurry up."

Frank, his temper flaring, dismissed her explanation. "She looks fine to me. I've seen her already this morning, and that boy of yours. I'll see you in my office at midday, and we'll find out if you're lying about Alice, too."

Katherine's heart chilled with dread, and she wished to avoid Frank's office at all costs. She was painfully aware of what happened in there.

"Just don't think about it or him," her colleague Milly whispered. Milly had witnessed Frank's harassment of Katherine and understood the torment she endured. She had been before him and had only managed to escape because Frank had moved on to Katherine. "Close your eyes and ignore him, and it'll be over before you know it. Don't answer him back, and he'll move on to his next victim."

But Katherine wasn't so sure. Frank seemed relentless, and she couldn't escape his advances. As she glanced up, she noticed Frank approaching another machine, leaving her to her anguish.

"What do you think you are doing?" Frank slammed his cane down on the floor three times.

"I'm—I'm sorry, sir."

"You're sorry? That's your wages docked! Pick the nails up off the floor and come to my office." Frank's dark eyes glared at the young worker who knelt on the floor, scratching around for every nail she had accidentally dropped.

The mill continued to churn out nails, oblivious to the drama unfolding within its walls. The deafening noise and noxious fumes filled the air, masking the suffering of its workers. A sudden, piercing scream resounded across the mill shattering the fragile peace.

Katherine's gaze snapped to where Grace was working, and both she and Peter raced to her side.

"Get up, child! Off that floor, clean yourself up, and get back to work," Frank bellowed, his fury evident.

Alice, tears streaming down her face, sobbed for her mother as she struggled to her feet, her clothes soiled.

"Alice? Alice, what's the matter?" Katherine rushed to her daughter, her heart pounding. "Are you okay?" Katherine knelt before her distressed child, desperate to soothe her. "Come on, let's get you home."

Frank, his eyes filled with disdain, intervened. "You will do no such thing. She can manage on her own. Now get back to work."

Katherine's blood ran cold as Frank grabbed her elbow forcefully. She pulled away, determined to take her daughter home.

"You will pay for this, Katherine," Frank hissed, his threat lingering in the air. "Get to my office now." He grabbed her by the elbow again and pulled her away from Alice.

Peter watched his ma being led away then turned his attention to his sister. "Come on, Alice, I'll help you," he said, trying to avert her attention of what was happening to their ma.

"Please don't, Mr Wilson, please. My daughter."

"Never mind, your daughter, there are plenty out there itching to get away from the machines to take good care of her."

The door slammed shut behind Frank and Katherine. "Don't you dare sit down, stand," he barked as he saw Katherine reach for a chair.

Katherine gazed towards the floor, unwilling to meet his eyes. "You owe me for that time lost, Katherine. How are you going to repay me? If I dock anymore of your wages, you won't be taking anything home, will you?"

"No—No, Mr Wilson, I won't."

"Very well, you will repay me in other ways then."

With his final words spoken to a shaking Katherine, he closed his office blinds and locked his door. Katherine found herself in the dimly lit office, her heart racing like a wild stallion out on the moors. The stern gaze of Mr Wilson bore into her, making her feel ashamed and as if she was on show in front of a thousand pairs of eyes.

She crossed her arms across her chest to make herself feel sheltered from his stare. "Yes, I will have to," Katherine stammered, her voice barely above a whisper. Mr Wilson leaned forward, his bushy eyebrows drawing together like thunderclouds.

"And why might that be?" His voice was a low rumble, sending shivers down Katherine's spine.

"I was late," Katherine replied, her fingers trembling as she clutched the edge of her shabby apron. He leaned back in his imposing leather chair. Katherine could feel his snake eyes run up and down her body.

"And why else might you be here?"

Katherine's heart sank, she could feel the weight of her own apprehension bearing down on her. "I don't know, sir," she admitted, her voice quivering.

"You don't know?" Mr Wilson's eyes bore into hers, searching for any sign of weakness. "Oh, I think you do, Katherine. You see, you've been ignoring my advances, haven't you?" His voice was a cruel whisper, dripping with accusation. "In fact, it seems to me you have been doing everything to avoid me. You helped Margaret when her machine got jammed this morning just to avoid me. You're nothing but heartless, Katherine, ignoring me. Heartless and cold. Can you guess what happens when I encounter a heartless and cold woman?"

As Frank Wilson rose from his desk and unfastened his belt buckle, Katherine bit her trembling bottom lip until it was bleeding. She closed her eyes, her heart pounding in her chest, and silently prayed for the shameful torment to be over.

"Now then," Frank Wilson said, his voice like a serpent's hiss, "get back to work, Katherine. If you're lucky, I might see you again later today;"

With a heart as heavy as lead, Katherine hurried out of his office, her steps quick but careful, as she dared not provoke further punishment. She made her way to her workstation, her hands trembling as she resumed her monotonous tasks. Some of the other women had gone to eat their dinner; the dinner bell had rung while she was in Mr Wilson's oppressive presence. But the thought of food made her stomach churn with nausea. She continued to toil away, counting the agonising minutes until the end of the day, when she could finally be with Edward and her children in the warmth and safety of their own humble home.

Chapter Six

After putting Alice to bed earlier, Katherine decided to rest by the fire and close her eyes until Edward returned home. She was overwhelmed with exhaustion and anxiety, her mind consumed by worries about Frank Wilson. She couldn't bring herself to confide in Edward, fearing his quick temper and jealousy. The last thing they needed was Edward storming into the mill, risking her job and their already precarious financial situation. What would they do if she lost her income? No, she thought it wiser to keep her troubles to herself, hoping Frank would soon find another unsuspecting target.

Peter slept upstairs with his sister, and as twilight descended and the room darkened, Edward finally stepped through the front door. His brow furrowed in confusion when he noticed Katherine asleep in the chair. He approached her quietly and gently planted a kiss on her forehead, his voice barely a whisper as he woke her from her slumber.

"Katherine, are you alright? Where are the children?"

Katherine awoke with a start, her eyes darting around as if disoriented. Hoping her senses would come to, she answered sleepily.

"They are in bed, they're tired and Alice isn't well. I'm worried about her."

Edward watched her with a puzzled expression as Katherine hurriedly ascended the stairs to their daughter's bedroom.

"I must have drifted off and didn't wake up." With a sense of urgency, Katherine flung open the bedroom door and rushed to her children's bedside. She gently shook them her voice trembling with worry. "Wake up, my loves, wake up."

Edward followed his wife upstairs, concern etched across his face. He stood in the doorway, his voice filled with anxiety. "What's wrong, Katherine, I don't understand. Can you please tell me what's happening?"

"Thank goodness!" she exclaimed, pulling her children close. "Alice has been unwell, Edward. She was sick at the mill earlier today, so I had to bring her home and put her to bed. I couldn't possibly leave her alone. When Peter returned home, he had a fever. I'm so worried about them both. I don't want them to go the same way as George," she said, hugging them tightly.

Edward's furrowed brow deepened, his worry evident. "But won't you lose your wages now?" he enquired.

Katherine's frustration flared up again as she glanced at her husband. "Edward, how dare you! Is that all you think about? Our children are ill and you're concerned about money? How could you, especially after losing George?"

Edward sighed, torn between his love for his family and the weight of their financial responsibilities. "I adore our children, you know I do. I couldn't even think about them getting sick like George did. Why would you believe that? But we still have bills to pay."

With a heavy heart, Katherine left the children to fall back to sleep and headed toward the bedroom door, her steps heavy with fatigue and exasperation. "I'm feeling exhausted, Edward. There's no dinner prepared, my wages are docked, and—"

"And what, Katherine? Are you going to talk to me?" Edward watched his wife walk further away from him, her every movement reflecting her exhaustion and frustration. Leaning on the kitchen table, he shook his head, grappling with his own worries and doubts. Katherine had been distant lately, not just tired but aloof, and he couldn't fathom the cause of her turmoil.

Perhaps Frank Wilson's actions were more tormenting than she had led him to believe, or maybe she was hiding something else entirely. Edward knew one thing for certain - he needed to find out the truth so that he could support his wife through whatever trials she faced.

Chapter Seven

Edward rolled over in bed towards his wife and whispered in her ear. "I'm sorry about last night, I will stay home today and look after them both. It will avoid giving the foreman a reason to complicate your life at the mill. And believe me, Katherine, I am so sorry, I promise never ever to speak to you like that again. I love you very much, you know. I will always love you, no matter what happens, we will always be fine, I just know it."

Katherine turned over to face her husband. "I know Edward, I just want it to be easier, that's all. The work at the mill was good to begin with, but since Mr Wilson started, it's just got worse."

"He's not harassing you is he?"

"No," Katherine responded sharply, pretending to be shocked by the notion of Frank harassing her, even though it was completely true.

"That's good because otherwise, he would have a piece of my mind, and maybe a punch to the guts. You get yourself to work and don't worry about supper, I will cook a broth, well I will try to cook."

"Now that, Mr Hartman, I would love to see!" Katherine said with a smile on her face as she got out of bed.

"Ma, I'm feeling okay today, I will come to work."

"Are you sure, Peter? You don't have to," she said. Although internally she had pleaded that at least one of them would be okay to work for the money.

"I'll be fine, ma, I promise."

Alice said goodbye to her husband then walked towards the mill with her son. She felt sick with nerves at the thought of being anywhere near Mr Wilson and his punishing ways. Anticipating the inevitable, she fought to avoid it, succumbing to trembling nerves and being sick by the side of the road. She took a handkerchief out of her pocket and wiped her mouth. *I wish I didn't have to see him today, or any other day for that matter.*

"Ma, are you okay? Are you sick now too?"

"No, Peter, I'm fine, it must have been supper last night. I'll be fine," she said meekly, smiling at her son and continuing towards the building of doom.

Approaching the mill she heard the familiar sound of the clanging of the machines, the acrid taste of metal from the nails in her mouth. With a battered heart, she loathed it, questioning if life would ever improve.

She kissed Peter goodbye and watched him walk towards the other children, clearing dust and grime from beneath and inside the machines. She wouldn't let her mind wander into a nightmare of envisioning her son getting killed one day because the machines had started up whilst he was trapped inside them.

No sooner had she sat at her machine and started working, Frank Wilson was behind her looking over her shoulder, like a nasty taste in her mouth. She could smell his breath and odour as he obviously hadn't washed this morning. You may have thought by looking at him he was smart in appearance, clean, and clever. But to Katherine, he was disgusting and rarely washed. She had to breathe through her mouth when he punished her so she didn't have to take in his odour too.

"Morning Katherine, I see you arrived on time today. Don't think that will save you. My office, midday!"

Katherine felt a tear come to her eye and as Milly walked past, she gave her friend a gentle squeeze on her wrist as if to offer her some form of comfort and sympathy.

Katherine's thoughts remained ensnared by the approaching midday ordeal, her heart heavy with dread, when an anguished scream rent the air, shattering her concentration. Her gaze snapped to the source of the commotion, just a few machines away. There, she witnessed a harrowing scene; a woman crumpled to the ground, the surrounding floor stained with a gruesome pool of crimson.

"Lord Almighty, someone help her!" Katherine's voice trembled as she called out, desperation welling up inside her. She couldn't stand idly by, not when a fellow worker's life hung in the balance. She rushed towards the fallen woman, her heart pounding like a drum. "Oh, no, please, not you, Betty. Come on, wake up!" Katherine reached her arm under her friend's neck and held her hand. She prayed for a miracle or help that would bring her dying friend around, but she knew it was helpless. The blood loss formed a pool on the factory floor, soaking into Katherine's clothes and staining her skin. She rocked her friend back and forth. "Please, Betty, can you not stay?"

Others in the mill responded too, their faces etched with concern and fear, their hurried footsteps echoing amidst the deafening clatter of machinery. Together, they knelt beside the stricken woman, their hands trembling as they sought to offer what little solace they could.

But their collective efforts proved in vain. Death had cast its unrelenting shadow, and the woman lay still, her life cruelly snatched away. A hushed lamentation filled the air, a mournful chorus of grief and disbelief. Katherine's thoughts raced, her mind haunted by the grim reality of this unforgiving place.

Tears welled up in Katherine's eyes as she considered the fate that had befallen a fellow worker and one of her closest friends. She couldn't help but picture her beloved Alice and Peter, the thought of a similar tragedy befalling her family sending shivers down her spine.

Across the mill, Frank issued his cold and calculated directives, orchestrating the cleanup as they awaited the undertaker's grim task. The anguished cries of the women pierced the air, their sorrow palpable.

Katherine longed to offer comfort, to share in their collective sorrow, but the menacing presence of Frank Wilson held her back, like a predator lurking in the shadows. Katherine locked eyes with the man who controlled her actions and advances at his whim. Feeling a heavy weight upon her chest, she knew she had to escape somehow, but dreaded the consequences if she was caught.

Chapter Eight

"Alice, how are you feeling?" Edward stroked his daughter's hair as he sat on the bed, cradling her like she was a baby again.

Unaware that her ma had left for the long gruelling hours at the mill, Alice had been asleep for most of the day. "I'm ok, pa, you make me feel better when you're around though."

Edward looked at his daughter and wished he could spend more time with her.

Alice had been barely eating lately, and he knew it was from working at the mill.

"Alice, are you well enough to get dressed and meet your mother from the mill? Let's surprise her shall we?"

"What do you mean, pa? I'm going to the mill today aren't I?"

"No, my love, you're not, you've slept right through but that doesn't mean we can't surprise your ma does it?"

Alice lifted herself off Edward and jumped down from the bed still feeling groggy.

Edward passed her some clothes and left her to get dressed on her own. "I'll see you downstairs, Alice, and perhaps you can help me make some broth for tonight."

"Okay, pa, I love you," she said groggily, rubbing sleep from her eyes.

"I love you too, Alice."

Edward went downstairs and walked over to the stove. *Now then, let's see if I know what to do with this.* He picked up a pot and put it down on the wooden table. He put a couple of pig's trotters and vegetables in the pot, Edward knew the ingredients tonight were a luxury and, may not be repeated if his business did not pick up soon. Just as Alice was coming downstairs, he filled the pot with water, put the lid on, and prepared to place it on the stove.

"Right then, Alice, the broth is ready to put on the stove so hopefully your ma will be pleased, let's go and meet her from the mill shall we?"

Alice and Edward donned their coats, with Edward grabbing his cap from the hook before leaving the house. He hoped it would give him some warmth on this cold, bleak day. He held Alice's hand, and they headed towards the mill. He knew that his wife had something on her mind, but she obviously didn't want to tell him. He thought by getting supper ready and meeting her from the mill might cheer her up a little, and they could try to talk again later when Alice and Peter were in bed.

"Pa, do you think ma will be pleased to see us?"

"I'm sure she will, Alice, who wouldn't be excited about seeing their beautiful daughter after a long, hard day? You always bring a smile to my face, that's for sure."

Edward hoped to make it up to Katherine. He felt guilty after speaking to her in such a way that dismissed how she felt about the children being sick. But he couldn't help it. The gentleman who had visited his workshop the day before had not returned to place an order, and Edward didn't know how to tell his wife. The truth was, that unless he made some money and fast, Edward would be in the mill too.

He looked at his daughter, and his heart melted. Edward would do anything to protect and provide for his family. He hoped that meeting Katherine and Peter from the mill would appease her so that she would be more amenable to Edward giving her the news that there were no new orders.

Edward watched Alice smile to herself and look down towards her feet as she started to skip a little, excited to see her ma and brother. As they approached the mill, Edward's heart started to race with anticipation.

Chapter Nine

Edward's heart pounded in his chest as he watched the scene unfolding before him. His beloved Katherine, the woman he adored above all else, was being accosted by someone he recognised right before his eyes. Anguish and confusion tore at his soul as he grappled with the reality of what he was witnessing.

Alice tugged at his hand, her innocent voice breaking through the chaos in his mind. "What are we doing, pa?"

"We—we need to hide," Edward whispered, his voice trembling with a mixture of fear and determination. He couldn't let Katherine see them, not like this. Not while she was in the clutches of that man, her distress palpable even from a distance. And where was Peter? Edward's breath quickened, he struggled to catch it as he wondered where his son was. The conspiracy theories circled around in his mind as to why his wife would be meeting this man without Peter there.

With a heavy heart, Edward led Alice away, his thoughts swirling with questions and doubts. How could Katherine allow herself to be treated in such a manner? What had driven a wedge between them, driving her into the arms of another? The weight of uncertainty bore down on him, threatening to crush him beneath its relentless pressure

As they sought refuge in the shadows, Edward's mind raced with possibilities. He couldn't confront Katherine now, not without knowing the full extent of what was happening. But he couldn't simply stand idly by either, watching helplessly as their lives unravelled before his eyes.

Clutching Alice's hand tightly, Edward made a silent vow to unravel the truth, no matter the cost. For if there was one thing he knew for certain, it was that he would do whatever it took to protect his family, even if it meant delving into the darkest depths of betrayal and deceit.

The sky was turning dusk and seemed to draw them in, enveloping them in its cold embrace. Edward felt like he had held his breath for minutes trying to catch a glimpse of movement close to the mill's entrance.

His heart lurched in his chest as he continued to watch Katherine walk alongside the stranger. His eyebrows furrowed as a glimpse of familiarity washed over him. He noticed the stranger trying to grab his wife's arm, and his stomach churned with a mix of dread and disbelief as he watched them draw nearer.

Alice's hand tightened in his own, her wide eyes reflecting the fear and uncertainty that gnawed at his own soul. "Pa, what's happening?"

she whispered, her voice barely audible above the pounding of his heart. "You look upset."

"Nothing—nothing. I just thought of something, that's all. But we must stay hidden, we don't want your ma to see us do we? It will spoil the surprise. I'm sure she will finish talking to that man soon."

Alice stood on tiptoe, trying to catch a glimpse of what her pa was talking about.

Meanwhile, Edward's gaze never left Katherine and the stranger. Every fibre of his being screamed for him to intervene, to confront them there and then. But he resisted, knowing that he needed more than just a fleeting glimpse to uncover the truth.

As he watched in silence, Edward's senses sharpened, his every instinct on high alert. He noticed the tension in Katherine's shoulders, the way she flinched away from the stranger's touch. And then, as if in slow motion, he saw the man's hand reach out, fingers curling around Katherine's arm with a force that made her wince.

A surge of fury surged through Edward's veins, his muscles tensing in readiness. But before he could act, Katherine met his gaze, her eyes widening in shock and horror. For a fleeting moment, their eyes locked, a silent plea passing between them before the stranger's grip tightened, dragging her away into the darkness.

Edward's heart shattered into a million pieces as he watched them disappear from view, his breath catching in his throat. And in that moment the weight of betrayal and despair threatened to consume him.

Chapter Ten

Edward stood frozen in the shadows, torn between the desire to intervene and the fear of making matters worse. His heart hammered against his ribs, each beat echoing the battle raging in his mind. Should he confront him, and risk escalating the situation, or should he wait for the perfect moment to rescue Katherine without putting her in further danger?

Could this man be the foreman that Katherine had talked about? Edward didn't want to put Katherine's mill work at risk, they desperately needed the money to put food on the table and pay the rent. Christmas was approaching and at the moment, the children would receive nothing more than a piece of stale bread and a Christmas carol around the fire.

His eyes stung with the acidity of his tears, but he refused to accept what was going on any longer. He didn't need to hesitate as he watched the man's grip on Katherine tighten, his intentions unmistakable. Edward's resolve hardened, his instincts screaming at him to protect his wife at all costs. With a silent prayer on his lips, he stepped out from the shadows, his presence like a thunderclap in the stillness of the night.

"Let her go," Edward's voice rang out, filled with a steely determination that brooked no argument. He swallowed down his fear and emotion, which felt like a cannonball in the back of his throat.

The foreman's eyes narrowed as he looked up, his grip on Katherine tightening even further as he turned to face Edward. "Glad to see you could make it, I wouldn't have brought your daughter though, she doesn't need to witness this."

"It's you! The stranger who came into the workshop yesterday wanting to place the big order."

"Yes, it was me, I wanted to know what I was up against to win your wife over. It doesn't look as if I need worry." Frank Wilson sneered, his voice dripping with disdain.

"I'm her husband," Edward declared, his voice trembling with suppressed rage. "And I won't stand by while you treat her like this, let go of her immediately."

Alice clung on to the back of her pa's trousers before running over to her ma and reaching out for her hand. She stuck her thumb in her mouth and glared at the foreman, who came across as a monster in front of her.

A tense silence hung in the air, thick with the promise of violence. Edward could see the anger simmering in Frank Wilson's eyes, the challenge unmistakable. And then, without warning, the foreman lunged forward, his hands grappling with Katherine as he tried to assert his dominance.

But Katherine fought back, her cries echoing in the night as she struggled against Mr Wilson's advances.

And in that moment, Edward knew that he couldn't stand idly by any longer. With a roar of defiance, he launched himself at the foreman, their bodies colliding in a flurry of fists and fury.

The sound of their struggle filled the air, mingling with Katherine's desperate pleas for help and Alice crying in the background. But Edward fought on, his every blow fuelled by the love he held for his wife. And then, in a moment of madness and anger, Frank's fist connected with Edward's jaw with a sickening thud.

Pain exploded behind Edward's eyes as he stumbled backwards, his vision swimming as he fought to stay conscious. But it was no use. Darkness closed in around him, swallowing him whole as he tumbled to the ground, his world spinning out of control.

As Edward lay there, battered and broken, Katherine screamed and her cries echoed around the outside of the mill and disappeared into the mist. "Noooo! What have you done?"

Frank Wilson looked at Katherine briefly, unable to open his mouth.

She looked at the foreman with cold, dark eyes and saw him hesitate over her husband's body.

He clutched his chest in shock as he held his mouth open, watching over Edward who wasn't moving. "I didn't—I didn't mean to do it," he whispered.

In a split second, Katherine grabbed her daughter's hand and ran as quickly as she could away from the scene in front of her. So fearful was she that he would then move on to her and Alice, and with her heart pounding in her chest, she had no alternative but to escape as quickly as her weak legs would carry her.

Looking on in the distance, young Peter became frozen to the spot. Unable to move, even to help his pa, he watched in disbelief as his ma and sister ran away. Within seconds, he could no longer see them. The young boy with threadbare shorts on, layers of ragged shirts and holy jumpers to keep him warm, had a feeling he would never see his family again.

Frank crouched down and put two fingers against Edward's neck. He shook his shoulders, willing him to wake up, then checked for his pulse again. *No! This can't be happening*, he thought as he looked around to make sure no one was watching. He considered his two choices quickly and in a fraught moment that he never expected to experience. And with his shallow breath and stone-cold heart, he stood up and walked away without looking back.

Chapter Eleven

"Come on, hurry, Alice. We must find him." Katherine gripped her daughter's hand tightly and lifted the trusses of her dress with another to enable her to run quicker.

"Find who, ma?"

"I'm talking about my brother, I'm sure he lives around here somewhere. He'll be able to help us."

The darkened, twisted streets and alleyways of Whitechapel seemed unfamiliar to Katherine and her daughter, who were used to living in a ramshackle and weather-beaten farmhouse. They had been walking for hours as quickly as possible to escape the nightmare they had witnessed.

Rosewood Cottage, the place they called home, which sounded so quaint and picture-perfect, was far away. Its rotten window frames, crumbling brickwork, damp ridden and murky walls were a distant memory and one that Katherine would do anything to get back. The house was nestled amidst the rolling hills of Willowbrook, a stone's throw away in a carriage, from the formidable streets of Whitechapel. Hours away if you were to walk and navigate the slippery and sludge covered cobbles. Katherine could only dream of returning to Rosewood Cottage one day. It may be close to falling down, but it had always made her feel safe.

As Katherine and Alice fled into the night, their hearts heavy with fear and uncertainty, Katherine's mind was a whirlwind of emotions. The image of her husband, Edward, lying battered and unconscious by the hands of the foreman haunted her every step. Tears welled in her eyes as she struggled to comprehend the sudden violence that had shattered their lives.

But there was no time to dwell on the horror of what had transpired. With Alice's hand tightly clasped in her own, Katherine pressed forward, each step a painful reminder of the sacrifices they were forced to make. As they ran through the dimly lit streets of Whitechapel, Katherine couldn't shake the feeling of being hunted, her senses on high alert for any sign of danger.

"Ma, it's getting dark, where are we going to sleep tonight? And where is Peter? He won't be able to find us!"

Katherine stopped in her tracks, put her hand on her hip, then looked around, sighing. "Who knows, Grace. I was hoping to find Alex, I just can't remember which street it is."

"What about Peter?"

"What about Peter?" Her shoulders dropped, and she felt the weight in her heart of her son who had been left behind. But tonight was about surviving as best as she could with her young daughter trailing behind her.

The woman looked around in desperation. "Excuse me, excuse me?" she said, walking up to a man with an A-Board on him advertising his useless wares.

"Aye? How can I help two young lasses like you? You shouldn't be out this time of night, these dark hours are only for people like me who are brave enough to endure them just to make a penny for some bread."

Katherine looked the man up and down. The patched-up holes in his clothes looked like they could be fixed again and for a moment, her heart softened, wondering who was at home waiting for him. "Erm—well—I'm looking for Linguard Street, am I far away?"

"If luck would have it, that's close to where I live. It might be the slums, but it's good enough for me. I'll take you there."

For the first time that day, Katherine felt a glimmer of hope, and she looked down at her daughter who was now smiling with anticipation. "That's very kind of you. I'm looking for my brother, Alex Compton, have you heard of him?"

"No, lass, I 'aven't, but let's see what we can do, shall we?"

Katherine followed the kind gentleman who looked like he would collapse any moment under the weight of the board. She continuously looked from left to right, and over her shoulder wondering if Frank Wilson would catch up. But for the moment, there was no sign.

"'Ere you go then, it's just down there," the ragpicker said.

"Thank you, thank you so much."

"It's no bother, I'm happy to help. If you don't find him, you can head on up the road and ask if there's a coffin bed or penny rope for the night." His eyes looked down at Alice and he shook his head then walked off.

Katherine smiled at him, then walked up the road to number 53.

"Where are we going, ma?"

"I've told you, Alice. Stop mithering, I need to concentrate."

Alice rubbed her eyes and her ma noticed she had started to cry.

"I'm sorry," Katherine said as she crouched down in front of her daughter, wiping her cheek with her thumb. "I know it's been a long day and night and we've both had a shock, but we need to find your Uncle Alex. Last time I heard, he lived on this street. He will help us."

Alice nodded, her tired eyes barely staying open.

Katherine and her daughter arrived at No. 53 and she took a deep breath before rapping on the door. *Please, Alex, be here,* she silently prayed for a miracle.

A child started crying and she heard the mother's cries. "Who's there now? I've nowt but a moment to spare, so speak your business quickly!" The door opened suddenly, Katherine didn't recognise the face.

"I'm sorry, I'm looking for Alex. Are you his—?"

"Who? I ain't 'eard of no Alex, and now you've woken my child, are you going to rock her back to sleep?"

"Please, I'm desperate. Have you seen him? I just need his help."

The young mother looked down at the tired, restless girl standing on her doorstep and felt a glimpse of empathy having been there herself. "I'm sorry, miss, I 'aven't heard of anyone called Alex. When did he live here?"

Katherine blew out her cheeks. "Are you sure? Last time I heard from him must have been ..." Katherine restlessly and impatiently tapped her foot, whilst searching for an answer in her fraught and muddled brain.

"Come on, 'urry up, I need to get back to my bairn. "

"It must be five years ago."

"Ha! You've no chance then, I've been here just less than that, he must have moved on without telling you. Sorry I can't help you."

The door unexpectedly slammed in Katherine's and Alice's faces. *What are we going to do now?*

With nowhere to go, and with each passing moment, the weight of their situation bore down on Katherine like a leaden cloak. She knew she had to keep moving, had to find a safe haven for Alice and herself, but the streets offered no solace, only the cold and their hunger gnawing at their bones.

Desperation clawed at Katherine's insides as she begged for scraps of food, her pride crumbling with each pleading word. "Please, sir, have mercy on a mother and her child," she implored, her voice hoarse with emotion. Each time she approached a stranger who looked as if they would have something to give, she loaded her voice with more emotion and frustration.

But they all turned a deaf ear to her pleas, their faces hardened by the harsh realities of life on the streets and their own worries and cares to weigh them down. And so Katherine pressed on, her determination unyielding despite the odds stacked against her.

As the night wore on and exhaustion threatened to consume them, Katherine's thoughts turned to finding shelter for the night. But with no money to spare, the task seemed insurmountable. "We'll find somewhere, Alice, I promise," she murmured, her voice a mere whisper in the chill night air.

But even as she spoke, doubt gnawed at Katherine's resolve. How could she protect her daughter without a roof over their heads? How could she keep her safe from the dangers that lurked in the darkness?

"Come on, let's see if we can get a bed for the night."

Katherine and Alice ran towards where the ragpicker told them there may be a bed. Looking both ways before running across the street, she then held Alice's hand tightly and headed for the slum house.

"What do you want?"

Katherine stumbled on her words at the sight of the man standing in front of her. He was smartly dressed, but something in his eyes told her that it was a front for his wicked and desperate ways.

"I'm—no, we—we are looking for a bed. Do you have one?"

The landlord looked her up and down and licked his lips.

Katherine rolled her eyes, hoping he wouldn't notice. "Please?"

"It's four pennies for the coffins or a penny for the ropes, your choice."

"But I haven't any money. I've had to flee," Katherine said as she moved her head to the side to look beyond the man at the door. She dreaded the thought of the mice, rats, and bugs joining her and her daughter in the small beds.

"Yeah, I bet you 'ave. You could always do me some favours as a means to pay."

Katherine felt sick to her stomach. "No thank you, we'll manage."

She turned on her heels and pulled a protesting Alice with her. Leaving the landlord watch them walk into the night.

Oh well, 'er problem not mine, there will be plenty more where she comes from. The landlord slammed the door and awaited his next slum dweller.

Chapter Twelve

※

As the moon cast its pale light upon the gritty streets of Whitechapel, Katherine and Alice found themselves in a dire predicament, their weary bodies huddled together against the biting cold of the night.

With every passing moment, the weight of their circumstances bore down upon them, leaving Katherine feeling utterly defeated, her heart heavy with despair.

As they sought refuge in the shelter of a dimly lit alleyway, Katherine's thoughts turned to the daunting prospect of spending the night on the unforgiving cobblestones. The distant sounds of revelry and laughter from nearby taverns only deepened her sense of isolation, reminding her of the stark contrast between their plight and the carefree lives of those around them.

With a heavy sigh, Katherine's gaze swept over Alice, her precious daughter who deserved so much more than the hardships they now faced. "I'm sorry, my love," she whispered, her voice barely audible above the din of the city. "I wish I could offer you more than this. We must find shelter, but it's not going to be nice."

"It's not going to be inside, is it?"

Katherine wanted to scream at her daughter with every fibre in her body that it wasn't her fault and she was doing the best she could. She thought her daughter was selfish when Katherine had risked so much and, lost her true love trying to save her. She knew that they would not be reunited with her son, Peter, unless they returned to the mill where the man who murdered her husband would probably welcome them with open arms. That was until he coercively turned on them again.

Katherine took a deep breath. "No, Alice. It won't be inside, but I wish we were with warmth from a fire and food inside us. I wish your pa and Peter were with us but they are not. For now, we are alone on the streets and we must keep each other warm."

Alice looked up at her ma with an empathetic understanding and, she made an agreement with herself that she wouldn't mither her ma again.

"Here, this will do." Katherine peeped around the corner into the ginnel that smelt of stale urine and was covered in small puddles of cloudy water between the cobbles. She looked up the passageway and found what she thought was a dry patch, and went to sit down. "You sit next to me and I'll keep you warm. I will give you my coat if you need it, but it's best we huddle in." Katherine lifted the hem of her dress and brought it to one side behind her legs. She didn't realise she was being watched intently.

"Don't!"

Katherine froze and looked around. "I'm sorry?"

"I said, don't, there must be better places for you to stay. Do you not have any money?"

Katherine grabbed her daughter's hand at the sight of the gentleman standing at the entrance to the ginnel. His silhouette was visible against the dusky light. She didn't want any more confrontations from presumptive men who wanted to do nothing but take advantage of her.

"It's none of your business, but if you must know, I'm waiting for someone."

The gentleman took his hat off and smiled. "No, you're not. I can tell. You were going to sleep there for the night and, in doing so, would subject yourself and your daughter to the beggars and triers who would come for you in the darkness. I wouldn't advise it if I were you."

Katherine's eyes were wide. "Who are you, and how do you know? You have no right to know my business!"

"Maybe not, but I do care. I can't offer you much but I can give you shelter."

"How much will that cost? I need to think of food tomorrow. It's just me and my daughter. My husband—he—he's dead." Tears started to flow freely from her red-rimmed eyes, the tears falling on her daughter's head as she held her tightly to her chest.

He didn't know where to look. Embarrassed at the vulnerability and grief that Katherine was showing, he didn't expect to be confronted with her tales of woe already. But he couldn't help but feel sorry for her. "I promise, you don't or won't owe me anything."

"What? Not even favours like the dirty old landlord of the slums asked of me?"

He shook his head and sighed with disbelief. "Nothing like that. Just a roof over your weary heads."

"But I don't understand why, you don't even know me. There are plenty of others you can help, so why us?"

In the dimly lit streets of Whitechapel, amidst the shadows and the cold, Nathaniel Westford found himself wondering how he could convince the woman and child under his roof so he could protect them from the destitution they faced. "Perhaps no one else wants help, it's not that I haven't offered."

Katherine looked from side to side and considered her options, then looked down at Alice who silently pleaded with her to accept the invitation.

"If it makes your decision any easier, I found myself destitute and alone on these very streets. It was a time of despair and desperation, a period marked by personal loss and hardship that tested me. My God I still miss her, but I have to move on."

Something in his words and tone of voice made Katherine believe him. Having just lost her husband she didn't know how she would continue without him and she understood the grief behind the words. Although the drama from a few hours earlier had slipped her mind, the will to survive had taken over. She hadn't grieved or considered for one moment what she would do with Edward.

"It was only because I encountered a kind-hearted soul who had offered me shelter and solace in my hour of need that I am here now. It was a gesture of kindness that left an indelible mark on my soul. I suppose you could say that it ignited something in me to pay it forward, to offer hope to those who found themselves in the same desperate circumstances I had once faced. I just have to look at those people to know they are going through the same thing that I did."

"I see. And how do I know that we will be safe and you're not just faking your story? You could be anyone. Do you hear me? Anyone! I hear that Jack the Ripper is doing his rounds." Katherine closed her eyes to try to blank out the detail that she heard in the gossip of the mill.

"Do you honestly think I would be helping you at this hour when I could easily be identified if I was Jack the Ripper? It's not completely dark just yet."

"I suppose, that's true."

Nathaniel flicked his head to the side and directed Katherine and Alice away from the dark, stinking ginnel onto the streets where their faces were illuminated by the faint glow of a nearby streetlamp.

With a heart full of empathy and understanding, Nathaniel extended his hand to Katherine and Grace, offering them a glimmer of hope amidst the shadows that threatened to engulf them. For in their eyes, he saw not only the reflection of his own past but also the promise of a brighter future, where acts of kindness could illuminate even the darkest of nights.

Chapter Thirteen

"Ma, I'm cold and I'm hungry. Why couldn't we go with that man?"

"It wasn't right, Alice, we didn't know him."

"But he seemed nice."

"I know he did, but after what we have been through, I'm finding it hard to trust someone right now."

Despite Nathaniel's pleas and offers to help, Katherine refused his charity at the last moment. "We will be fine," she had said. The conflict of wanting to accept the help but not trusting the stranger had torn at her soul, but she couldn't go with him.

As the last vestiges of daylight faded from the sky, leaving the streets of Victorian London shrouded in darkness, Katherine huddled with her daughter, Alice, in the shelter of a narrow alleyway. The chill of the evening air seeped through the threadbare fabric of their coats, sending shivers down their spines as they clung to each other for warmth.

For two long nights, they had sought refuge in the shadows, their stomachs empty and their spirits worn thin by the harsh realities of life on the streets. Katherine's heart ached with despair as she looked down at Alice, her precious daughter, her face pale and drawn with exhaustion. How had it come to this so quickly? Only a few days ago, despite feeling desperate for food and wondering how they were going to pay the following month's rent, at least she had Edward and Peter. How had they fallen so far from the life they had once known? One name. Frank Wilson. He had destroyed their life and Katherine didn't know what she was going to do.

As the darkness deepened, so too did the dangers that lurked in the alleys and lanes of the city. The threat of the workhouse loomed large again in Katherine's mind, a spectre of fear that haunted her every waking moment. She had heard the stories whispered among the destitute and downtrodden, tales of cruelty and hardship that awaited those who dared to seek shelter within its walls. The harsh reality of a workhouse in Whitechapel sounded far worse than the mill at Willowbrook.

And then, as if summoned by her darkest fears, a figure emerged from the shadows, his footsteps echoing loudly against the cobblestones. A stranger with a twisted face and cruel sneer laid eyes upon Katherine and Alice.

"Well, well, what do we have here?" he sneered, his voice dripping with malice as he advanced towards them. "A pair of runaways, eh? Thought you could escape the clutches of the workhouse, did you?"

Katherine's heart pounded in her chest as she pulled Alice close, a surge of fear coursing through her veins. "Please, sir, we mean no harm," she pleaded, her voice trembling with desperation. "We're just trying to survive."

But the man's laughter cut through the night air like a knife, sharp and cruel. "Survive? You call this survival?" he scoffed, his gaze sweeping over Katherine and Alice with disdain. "Come with me, woman. You and the girl. You'll find shelter and a warm meal at the workhouse."

Panic surged through Katherine as the man reached out to grab her arm, his grip like iron as he tried to pull her away. With a surge of strength born from desperation, she wrenched herself free, her heart pounding in her chest as she grabbed Alice's hand and fled into the darkness.

For hours, they darted through the labyrinthine of streets, the sounds of pursuit echoing in their ears as they sought refuge from their would-be captor. But as exhaustion threatened to overcome them, Katherine knew they couldn't keep running forever. She wished with all her heart that she had accepted Nathaniel's offer of help, that she hadn't let her pride stand in the way of their survival.

As dawn broke over the city, casting a golden glow across the rooftops, Katherine's heart sank with despair. They had spent the entire day searching for Nathaniel, scouring the streets and alleyways in a desperate bid to find him. But as the day drew to a close and darkness descended once more, she found herself back where it all began, in the shadowy depths of the alleyway.

"Ma, I'm not sure I can walk today, I'm so tired."

"So am I, Alice, but we have to keep moving." Katherine thought back to the night when Nathaniel had appeared through the smog like a guardian angel. Now she deeply regretted saying no. "How about we keep trying to look for that man again? Maybe he will help us, and this time I won't say no!"

Alice perked up a little. "Can we, ma, can we?"

"Oh I see," she said smiling, "happy enough to walk a little to find that nice man are you?"

Alice looked away. Embarrassed.

"I'm just teasing, Alice, come on, let's walk awhile."

Katherine and Alice walked from street to street, occasionally slipping on the grimy cobbles and looking hopefully for edible scraps that had been thrown onto the streets. Katherine felt exasperated and resorted to spending another night on the streets. They huddled together, dozing in and out of unconsciousness from starvation and exhaustion.

"Hello again, still here I see?"

Katherine mustered any ounce of strength she had to sit up straight and smile.

"I thought I might find you still here, let me help, please. Look at you both, you look dreadful. I'd be surprised if you survived another night."

Tears welled up in Katherine's eyes as she rushed forward to meet him, relief flooding her senses at the sight of him. "I'm so sorry. I should have accepted your help sooner."

"There's no need for apologies," he murmured, his voice soft and reassuring. "All that matters is that you will both be safe now."

Chapter Fourteen

Katherine and Alice stepped into Nathaniel's humble abode, the weight of grief hung heavy upon them, and a palpable presence was in the air that seemed to suffuse every corner of the room. The flickering glow of the hearth cast dancing shadows across the worn but welcoming furnishings, lending a sense of solace to their weary souls.

Nathaniel, ever the attentive host, offered them a warm smile as they settled into their newfound sanctuary. "Please, make yourselves at home," he said, his voice gentle yet commanding. "You must be weary from your wanderings." He knelt down in front of the fire and poked it to ignite the flames, a couple more lumps of coal joined the burning embers in the grate. "First things first, though. What shall I call you?"

Katherine thought for a moment, she was terrified her past would catch up with her, or more importantly, Frank Wilson. "I'm Kitty, this is my daughter, Grace."

Alice's eyebrows furrowed together in confusion. When Nathaniel turned around to stoke the fire, Katherine looked at Alice and put her finger to her lips. "Shh," she whispered into her daughter's ear. "That's who we are now."

Alice looked at her ma with a level of understanding that they wouldn't speak about their change of identity ever again.

"And you, what shall we call you?"

"Oh, yes. Nathaniel Westford, call me Nathaniel."

Kitty managed a grateful nod, her eyes betraying the weariness that gnawed at her spirit. "Thank you, Nathaniel," she murmured, her voice barely above a whisper. "We are truly grateful for your kindness." She looked around warily and wondered what and who was behind each door. "Does anyone else live with you?" She noticed Nathanial stop what he was doing and look at her. "I'm sorry, that was rude of me."

"Not at all. I just have my son, Archie."

"Oh," Kitty said, looking around.

"You sound surprised."

"No, it's just that there seems to be a lot of rooms here."

Nathaniel went back to stoking the fire and hesitated before he answered. He stood up and walked over to the stove. "Would you and your daughter like some hot tea?"

"I don't want to put you to any trouble."

"It isn't. Besides, I offered you a bed for the night. Cups of tea with a place to sleep go hand in hand." Nathaniel studied Katherine's features as she looked away. He felt his heart beating a little faster than normal, but he pushed the feeling aside. It wasn't appropriate for him to have such feelings when he should still be grieving for his wife.

"In which case that would be wonderful."

The sound of her delicate voice brought Nathaniel back to the room. Never had he heard such sweetness and charm from a woman who looked like she had been homeless for weeks. Nathaniel directed Kitty with his hand towards a chair by the fire.

"Do you mind me asking, how old is your son?" Kitty settled into the seat. The silence of the room when neither of them spoke seemed to press in around them, a stark reminder of the emptiness that now filled her precious and broken heart.

Nathaniel watched her closely, his gaze filled with a quiet understanding born of his own experiences with loss. "Archie is ten, he's growing up to be a fine young boy, I have high hopes for him."

Kitty wondered what made Nathanial say that.

As Nathanial was making tea, a door opened and a boy of about Grace's age, offered a shy smile from across the room, his eyes curious yet kind. "Hello," he said softly, his voice tinged with the innocence of youth.

Grace, sitting by her ma, hesitantly returned his smile, her own grief mirrored in the depths of her eyes. "Hello," she replied, her voice filled with a mixture of apprehension and longing.

As Kitty watched the two children interact, a pang of grief washed over her, reminding her of the son she had been forced to leave behind. Peter, her eldest, was still at the mill, his fate uncertain in the wake of their sudden departure.

When Nathaniel looked over at the woman he had rescued from the murky streets, he noticed the sadness that clouded Kitty's eyes, his heart aching for her in her time of need. "I'm sorry for your loss," he said softly, his words heavy with empathy. He passed the tea to her. "I too know the pain of losing a loved one."

Kitty nodded, her throat tight with emotion. "My husband—he was taken from us," she whispered, her voice barely audible above the crackling of the fire. "I don't know who to trust anymore, or why I should stay."

Nathaniel's gaze softened, his own grief mirrored in her eyes. "I understand," he replied, his voice filled with compassion. "But know that you are safe here, that you and Grace are welcome for as long as you need."

"But I still don't understand. Why us? Why are you being so kind?"

"Do you have to understand? Or is it better to rest your weary mind and aching limbs and just accept that maybe someone is watching over you? I want you to know the offer to stay has come from the goodness of my heart, nothing else." He smiled graciously.

Kitty yawned and stretched her arms above her head.

"You look exhausted, why don't I show you both your room? Archie and I have to be up early anyway."

"Are you working tomorrow?"

"I am. I'm the headmaster at the school on Greengate Lane, the largest ragger's school in the area. Don't look surprised," he said, noticing Kitty's jaw dropping slightly.

"Sorry, it's just I wouldn't have expected you to work at a school." Kitty gazed around the humble room with its second hand furnishings.

"If you're wondering, I don't get paid very much. And some of what I do get—well—I give to those in need."

"That's very kind of you. Have you always worked there?"

"No, only since Agatha died. Before that I served in the Crimean War. Then when my wife passed, I wanted to do something more meaningful. Life is so short isn't it," he looked away and Kitty thought she saw a tear in his eye illuminated by the flames of the fire.

"Yes, it is," she said, remembering the traumatic events of earlier in the day.

"I'm sorry, that was heartless of me."

"Please, don't apologise, there is no need. You have been so kind and we have only just met. You can be forgiven for forgetting what we have been through these past few days."

"You can tell me more if you want, I promise I won't say a word. I'll just listen intently and only speak if you want me to."

Kitty looked at the guardian angel sitting opposite her with his tall frame, handsome good looks, and jet black hair. His piercing brown eyes lit up with the flames from the fire reflecting brightly within.

The fire crackled merrily in the hearth and the shadows danced upon the walls, and Kitty forgot all about her tiredness. She found herself opening up to Nathaniel in a way she hadn't thought possible. In his quiet strength and unwavering support, she found a lifeline amidst the storm of her grief, a beacon of hope in the darkness that threatened to consume her.

And as Nathaniel listened, his innate ability to offer comfort and solace shining through, Katherine knew that she had found not only a place to rest her weary body but also a kindred spirit to share the burden of her sorrow.

Chapter Fifteen

"Are you sure you want to do this?"

"Yes, it's the best thing for Grace, and I know Archie will look after her."

Grace looked down towards her feet at the second hand shoes and passed down school uniform.

Two weeks on and Kitty knew she had to get Grace back to some normality. As much as it broke her heart to be separated from her daughter, it was the best thing for her. "Don't look so glum, Grace. Meeting other children and learning your arithmetic and English will stand you well in life. I won't have you working in a mill, I don't want that future for you. Go to school and get educated and you will be able to do anything you put your mind to."

"But, ma, what if that horrible man comes?"

"Who? Mr Wilson? He won't, I will be safe here." Kitty hoped that her daughter wouldn't recognise the hesitancy in her voice.

Grace nodded, and Archie reached out for her hand.

"Come on, I'll show you the way."

"This is so kind of you, Nathaniel. I didn't expect any of this."

It had been a long two weeks for Katherine and Grace. Katherine had to accept that Edward had died, she was too scared to go back to the mill to look for Peter, and life needed to carry on. By switching things off in her mind, she could focus on what she was going to do next.

"It's no trouble, I work there anyway, and I'm sure Archie will be pleased to have a new friend, won't you?"

His son hadn't heard him. Already, the two children were heading out of the door hand in hand.

"I must do something for you, please."

Nathaniel sighed. "Alright, if it makes you feel better, why don't you clean and do the laundry today? I may be a little later with the children tonight so perhaps you could cook supper too. That would be so helpful." He walked over to a shelf next to the stove and reached up for a battered tin. He took some coins out and passed them to her. "Here, use these to buy what you need."

Kitty's eyes lit up. It had been a long time since a man had provided for her. It made her feel safe and secure knowing that she was unlikely her or Grace would go hungry again. "Thank you, I don't know what to say."

Nathaniel looked at her with a promise behind his eyes that he would always protect and care for her.

Kitty turned away, unwilling to admit she could feel a glimmer of heartfelt hope and warmth so soon after losing Edward.

Nathaniel, Archie, and Grace walked hand in hand down the street towards the ragger's school where the poorest and filthiest of children, both orphaned and parented, were educated. Nathaniel smiled as he said hello to some parents he recognised, many of whom had a lot of time for the school headmaster, knowing he was doing right by their children.

"Mornin' Mr Westford, you have a new pauper with you today I see?"

"Good morning Mrs Heathly, she's a bright young girl who has a talented future and if I can help, then so be it." Nathaniel knew to cut off any unnecessary negativity or gossip before it started. And seeing that he had a woman and child staying with him, he knew it wouldn't be long before the stories and whispers of how Kitty and Grace came to be at his house would hit the streets of Whitechapel. He continued along the cobbles tapping his long umbrella firmly in time with each long-legged stride.

Mrs Heathly nodded once, smiled, and went on her way.

"Right, Grace. I want you to stick by Archie today. I will put you in the same class, keep quiet, listen to the teacher, and do your best."

"Yes, sir."

"And please, you must stop calling me that. I will think of something more suitable later."

The headmaster walked towards Mrs Mason's classroom. "Good morning, Mrs Mason."

The teacher lifted her hands in the air to the children who were sitting quietly in their seats, signifying for them to stand and greet the headmaster.

"Good morning, Mr Westford," they said in unison before Mrs Mason lowered her hands back down, silently instructing the children to sit again.

"Who do we have here?" She asked, looking at Grace. "And good morning Archie, don't worry about being late, it looks like your pa has his hands full this morning."

Archie ran off and took his seat next to John and, a small amount of chatter passed between the two young boys before Mrs Mason looked over and gave them a cold, hard stare. They stopped talking instantly and sat ridged on the hard bench.

"This is Grace. She is staying for a while and so I have suggested she comes to learn with Archie, you don't mind, do you?"

"Not at all, why don't you sit next to Victoria, there is a spare seat." Mrs Mason touched Grace gently on her back guiding her toward a young girl sitting on the end of a bench.

"Be wary please, Mrs Mason. The young girl lost her pa a couple of weeks ago. She hasn't quite come to terms with it. It's doubtful she will be reunited with her younger brother and her ma is—I would say—bereft and grieving."

"Oh, Mr Westford, that's terrible," the teacher brought a hand up to her mouth to stop the emotion from pouring out of her soul. She had worked at the school for as long as it had been open and was known as the mother of the school. She had a welcoming heart and a big, cuddly, soft frame for children to bury themselves into when they needed to shed a tear. "Leave her with me, I will see that she is taken care of."

"Thank you, Mrs Mason, I appreciate it." Nathaniel turned around and headed for his office along the cold, stark corridor leaving Mrs Mason wondering how he had gained a new family practically overnight.

"Who are you then?"

Kitty caught her breath and turned at the sound of a gruff and unnecessary loud female voice.

"I'm sorry, are you talking to me?"

"Of course I'm talkin' to you, there ain't no one else around is there?"

Kitty averted her eyes doing a full turn hoping to find someone else who the stranger might be talking to. "Kitty, I'm new around here."

"I can tell, I ain't seen you before. Actually, I tell a lie. I've seen you out and about with that handsome school master, Mr Westford. Every woman around 'ere wants a piece of 'im, I can tell ya."

Katherine blushed. "Oh, well, I know he's a widower, but I'm not sure he's looking for love."

"You're posh for round 'ere, where've you come from?"

"Willowbrook, do you know it?"

"Yeah, I 'eard of it alright. What brings you round 'ere then and are you with Mr Westford now? He's broken lots of women's 'earts he has."

"No! No! I am not with Mr Westford in that way whatsoever. I'm a grieving widow having just lost my husband two weeks ago. Mr Westford has kindly offered us a place to stay whilst we get back on our feet."

"Is that right?"

"Yes, yes, that's right."

"We'll see about that. I reckon now he has you he's not gonna let you go. You're the prettiest thing that's been around 'ere for a while."

"I can assure you that won't happen," Kitty said, growing increasingly impatient with the stranger.

"Tell Mr Westford I'm asking for him won't ya?"

"What's your name? I can't tell him that without you telling me who you are."

"Audrey's the name, he'll know me." The red faced, big bosomed woman smiled at Katherine then turned around and walked off.

How dare she think I'm that way inclined, I've never heard such nonsense. Katherine could lie to herself all she wanted, but she couldn't ignore the feeling she had for Nathaniel no matter how deep she tried to bury it. But with many things playing on her overloaded mind, Kitty didn't notice the person lurking in the shadows.

Chapter Sixteen

Earlier that day, as Kitty had watched Grace and Archie walk hand in hand towards the ragger's school, a mixture of emotions swirled within her. Gratitude for Nathaniel's kindness warred with anxiety over her daughter's well-being in this unfamiliar environment. She couldn't shake the worry that lingered in the pit of her stomach, a gnawing fear born of recent losses and newfound vulnerabilities.

"It's no trouble, I work there anyway, and I'm sure Archie will be pleased to have a new friend, won't you?" Nathaniel's reassurance had broken through Kitty's thoughts, offering a fleeting sense of comfort amidst her turmoil.

But even as they parted ways, a shadow of doubt lingered in her mind. Was she doing the right thing by allowing Grace to attend school? Shouldn't she keep her close, protect her from the dangers that lurked in the world outside?

Kitty busied herself cleaning and scrubbing and doing the laundry. She pressed the dolly into the tub and twirled it around with all her might until the clothes were wrapped around the long handled wooden washing peg. A swirl of emotions caught up with her as she thought about her husband and son. The shock took over and, as she rested the standing dolly in the tub, she almost collapsed backwards onto an upturned barrel.

She found herself consumed by worry, her thoughts drifting back to the events that had brought her to this moment. Losing her husband, the uncertainty surrounding Peter's fate, and now, the decision to entrust Grace's safety to a stranger weighed heavily upon her heart.

As the day wore on, the autumn sun in the sky started to fade and she wondered what tomorrow would bring.

"Hello, Kitty? We're home." Nathaniel led the children inside the house. They each took their coats off and hung them behind the door. "Let's go and see where your ma is and tell her what happened."

Grace wiped her eyes, a smudge of blood catching her thumb and then transferring to her dress as she wiped her snotty and tear covered hand on the front of her dress.

"Don't worry, Grace, you will be fine." Archie reached out his hand for hers and she took it without a second hesitation.

"Kitty, where are you?" Nathaniel walked through to the kitchen and then to the stove, standing over the pot bubbling away. He wafted the smells towards his nose with his hand and breathed in deeply. *That smells delicious*, he thought before heading upstairs to find Kitty.

"Kitty?" he whispered at the bedroom door, knocking lightly. "Can I come in?"

There was no answer, so he knocked again gently. With no sign of his new friend stirring he quietly opened the door and saw her lying asleep on the bed. The patchwork quilt was ruffled around her feet, her clothed body exposed to the chill in the air. Nathaniel stood over her and wondered whether to sit beside her on the bed. Instead, he pulled the quilt over her and covered her shoulders.

Kitty's eyes gently opened gently, then, suddenly dawning on where she was, she sat up, leaning on her elbow. "Grace! Where is she?"

Nathaniel touched her shoulder gently. "She's fine, well, almost. I don't want you to be concerned, but there has been a bit of an incident."

The worried mother shoved the quilt away, her feet getting tangled in it. Then she swung her legs over the side of the bed and stood up. She swayed slightly and touched her forehead.

"Are you alright?" he said, tenderly reaching out to catch her.

Kitty's heart melted. "Yes, yes, I'm fine. Where is she?"

"Come with me."

They both hurried down the stairs and, noticing the cut on her head, Kitty rushed towards her daughter. "Grace! What happened," she said, crouching down in front of her young daughter.

"Two children didn't like me," Grace said, wiping her eyes again.

"What do you mean? Why didn't they like you?"

"If I can explain, Kitty. Grace got into a small altercation at school with two other children, I actually think they came off worse thanks to Archie."

Kitty glanced over at the young boy. "Are you hurt as well, Archie?"

Nathaniel couldn't help but notice the nurturing mannerisms that came naturally to the woman he met only a few weeks ago.

"No, not really. I'm fine."

She turned her attention back to her daughter and sighed deeply. "This is not good news. I think we should leave, I knew I shouldn't have let her go. It's too soon."

"Wait a minute, it was just one incident and it's been dealt with. They have been reprimanded by Mrs Mason, it won't happen again, I promise you." Nathaniel said hastily.

"Go to your room, Grace, I will be up in a moment."

"You too, Archie," Nathaniel said, instinctively sensing that Kitty wanted to talk in private.

The two children sloped off feeling sorry for themselves, as both parents watched them leave.

Kitty put her hands on her hips. "We have to leave, I can't have this for Grace. It's hard enough her trying to come to terms with the loss of her pa, and she's missing Peter too, it's not fair on her."

"Don't leave based on what happened. I promise she won't be subjected to that kind of attention again."

"Listen to you all high and mighty and acting like a hero. I'm not impressed, Nathaniel and we should never have stayed."

"But—"

"But what? You want me to come running into your arms hoping you will rescue me? I won't, I'm still grieving, and to be led astray by a stranger and for things to move so quickly for Grace is—well, it's unacceptable and inappropriate."

"But, Kitty, please, I'm just trying to help. The last thing I wanted was for Grace to get hurt. It wasn't intentional, I promise."

"Maybe not, but it doesn't change the situation does it? We are both grieving, Grace has moved too quickly into a school where she is quite clearly not accepted by the other children, and we are—we are homeless and have lost the only people we ever loved." Suddenly, her bottom lip started trembling, and she burst into tears. She felt for the seat behind her and sat down.

"Kitty, please," Nathaniel said, rushing over and kneeling down in front of her. His hands were firmly on his thighs to avoid touching the most beautiful, kindest woman he had ever laid eyes on since his wife had died.

"I think it's best if we leave. I've had all I can take today. Not only did that happen to Grace, but that woman from across the road, what's her name?" She glanced up slightly towards the ceiling whilst her mind flicked through the library of stored memories and names in her head. "Oh yes, Audrey!"

Nathaniel sighed and rolled his eyes before Kitty continued.

"Apparently you break women's hearts and she made out you've had a few since your wife died."

"It's not true, she's nothing but trouble. I will have a word with her tomorrow."

"Whether it's true or not, it's another thing I can't deal with right now. Grace and I are leaving tomorrow and that's final." Kitty stood up, leaving Nathaniel kneeling absentmindedly on the floor. "Supper is cooking, I don't want any." She walked out of the door and up to the bedroom to find Grace.

Nathaniel closed his eyes and shook his head slowly. *But I like you Kitty, why can't you see that? I just want to protect you.*

"What's wrong, pa, what's happened?"

"Not much, son. But Kitty and Grace are leaving tomorrow," he said, standing up and ruffling his son's hair.

"I like them, it's been nice whilst they have been here."

"I agree, Archie, but we can't have everything can we? Our happiness wasn't meant to last. We'll just have to let them go."

Grace walked into the room, her bleeding head cleaned and her hair had been brushed. "Ma said I should eat something." She walked over to where Nathaniel was standing in front of the stove then sat down next to her friend, Archie. "I don't want to leave, I like it here. I've felt safe while me and ma have been here."

"You've got to do what your ma tells you, Grace. You must respect her. I know it will be sad, but maybe we can meet again someday."

Outside the room, Kitty was listening with her ear resting on the other side of the door. She stood, biting her nails, listening to how her daughter didn't want to go. She couldn't help but notice the soft, loving, and warm tones of Nathaniel's voice, and Archie's soothing words. *Maybe I've been hasty and stupid, it wasn't Nathaniel's fault. I'm just scared.*

Kitty felt guilty for shouting at the one gentleman who had watched out for her since running from the mill. She had been too quick to judge him and blame him for something that wasn't his fault. All in the name of protecting her and Grace from any further harm. One thing was for sure though, she couldn't go back on her word. That would mean apologising and likely falling in love. She had already had inappropriate feelings and thoughts for someone she had only met a few weeks ago when she barely knew him. She took a deep breath in, pierced her lips together, then walked back up the stairs feeling too proud to walk in and ask for supper. Tomorrow she would rise early and leave with her daughter.

But even as the thought crossed her mind, Kitty knew that running away wouldn't solve anything. She knew she should stay, to face her fears head-on and protect her daughter from the cruelties of the world. For in the depths of her grief, she found a newfound strength, a determination to fight for the happiness and safety of those she loved. But she was too embarrassed and stoic to dream of staying any longer.

Chapter Seventeen

"Come on, Grace, hurry. We must leave now." Kitty tried her best to rouse her daughter from her sleeping slumber, but Grace was tired after the events of the day before.

Grace slowly came around and sat up in bed. "Ma, I don't want to leave. Archie is my friend, and he doesn't want me to leave either. Why can't we stay?"

"Because, Grace, it's not safe here. We didn't escape that horrid man for you to be bullied at school. We must move on."

"But it won't happen again, Archie said he will watch out for me."

"That won't stop the bullying, Grace. Now, get ready, we have to go. I won't ask you again."

"Can I have some tea, please? Then I promise I will get dressed."

Kitty sighed then walked downstairs shuffling her way to the kitchen. She filled the whistling kettle with water and placed it on the stove. She rested her hands on the table to take a few moments to gather her strength. As the kettle whistled its merry tune, she awoke from her thoughts and turned around. Noticing the piece of paper on the small table by the door, she frowned and unfolded it, having seen her handwritten name on the front.

'My Dearest Kitty,

As I sit down to write this letter, my heart is heavy knowing that you and Grace will soon be leaving us. The days we have spent together, though fleeting, have brought a light into my life that I never knew was missing. Your presence in our home has brought warmth and joy, casting aside the shadows of grief and loneliness that once clouded our hearts.

I cannot begin to express my sorrow at the thought of saying goodbye. From the moment you walked through our door, you captured my imagination and filled my thoughts with dreams of a future filled with laughter and love. Your strength in the face of adversity, your unwavering devotion to your daughter, and your boundless compassion have touched me in ways I cannot fully articulate.

I know that you are still grieving, that the wounds of loss are still fresh and raw. And yet, despite your pain, you have brought happiness and hope into our lives. For that, I am eternally grateful. You and Grace have become a part of our family, and the thought of parting ways fills me with a sadness I cannot bear.

But I understand that you must do what is best for you and your daughter. You have faced hardships that few can imagine, and I would never presume to stand in the way of your journey towards healing and happiness. Know that wherever life may take you, my thoughts and prayers will always be with you.

I wish you nothing but the best, Kitty. May the road ahead be filled with love, laughter, and endless blessings. And though our paths may diverge for now, I hold on to the hope that someday, our paths will cross once more. Until then, know that you will always have a place in my heart.

With all my love and deepest affection,
Nathaniel'

Kitty watched a tear drop to the table. She pulled the cuff of her sleeve over her hand and wiped it away. She sighed deeply and shook her head then poured the tea and took a cup up to her daughter.

"Thanks, ma."

Kitty sat on the side of her daughter's bed and stroked her hair. "I love you, Grace. Everything I do from now on is for you, I just want you to know that."

Grace slurped her hot tea and smiled at her. "I don't really want to go."

"Neither do I, but we must. We have to find our own way now after what happened. I simply can't turn around to Nathaniel and Archie and tell them we are staying."

"Why, ma?"

"Because it wouldn't be right or fair on any of us. We all need to know where we—" Kitty froze. "Is anyone there? Did you hear anything, Grace?"

"Perhaps it's Nathaniel and Archie coming home to tell us to stay."

Kitty ignored the heartfelt hope from her daughter and tiptoed downstairs. She reached the bottom step after hearing what she thought was a sound coming from the kitchen. *That's strange, I'm sure I turned the stove off.* Thinking nothing more of it, she walked straight through to the kitchen when suddenly an arm grabbed her from behind, reaching in front of her neck. Another hand clasped over her mouth. As much as she tried, a sound wouldn't leave her lips.

"I found you, Katherine. Did you think you could escape me?"

Frank Wilson dragged her over to the sofa and roughly threw her down. "Don't you say another word, do you hear me?"

Kitty's blood ran cold and her heart raced into her throat. "Don't hurt me, please."

"I said be quiet!" A hand slapped across the young mother's face, shunning it to the side.

Kitty reached for where she had felt the slap, her hot red skin burning in her fingers.

"Thought you could escape, did you? Not from me. In case you're wondering, I've been keeping an eye on you and had you followed. You're coming with me!"

"No, she's not!"

"Gr —," Kitty hesitated briefly, remembering they had changed their names in the hope Frank Wilson would never find them. "Alice, go away, go back upstairs and shut your door," Kitty cried.

"No, I'm staying here with you, ma. Leave us alone you horrible man."

Frank Wilson laughed and sneered as spittle left his mouth. "Not a chance. You're both leaving with me now." He pulled Kitty up and grabbed Grace by the arm.

"Ow you're hurting me!" Grace cried.

"Shut up, you little—"

"Please, Frank, leave us alone. I promise I won't say anything."

"I don't trust you, we're leaving." Frank pushed them both towards the door, almost knocking them over on top of each other. He reached forward and turned the handle.

"What the—?"

"Nathaniel!" Kitty had never felt so relieved. All her embarrassment and guilt washed away as her tears fell fast and heavy and her body started shaking.

"Who are you?" Nathaniel shouted.

"None of your goddamn business, get out of my way."

"Anything that involves these two is my business, get out of my house." Nathaniel grabbed Frank and pushed him towards the door, but Frank was heavier and bulkier, his large frame looming over Nathaniel.

Frank punched Nathaniel in the eye socket as Kitty and Grace cried out. "Stop it, please?"

Kitty watched the drama unfold in front of her and, her vision of Edward being knocked to the ground replayed in her mind. She thought that Frank was going to kill Nathaniel too and would stop at nothing to get what he wanted. She watched helplessly as Nathaniel struggled to get up, but then saw him look to the side.

The fire iron was lying just outside Nathaniel's reach. In an instant, Katherine flung herself towards it, took it in both hands and hit Frank across his back. He cried out in pain, reaching for where he had been struck with both hands. Then she hit him hard against the back of his knees.

"I suggest you leave, now!" Nathaniel shouted.

For a moment, Kitty thought Frank would fight back, finding resolve and strength in his determination to take her. But, she saw him stare in her eyes before walking towards the door. She breathed a sigh of relief, then it felt like her heart leapt into her mouth as Frank turned around.

"I haven't finished with you yet, Katherine, I will come back for you." Then, he walked out of the house leaving the door open, Nathaniel on the floor, and Grace crying like she had never done before.

Nathaniel looked confused at Kitty as she reached out a hand and helped him up.

"Katherine? Why did he call you Katherine?"

"Oh, it's my full name, and I shortened it in the hope he wouldn't find me. Not that it did much good.

"Kitty, listen to me. I will never ever let that man near you, I promise." He reached out to the terrified woman in front of him and pulled her close, feeling her melt into his arms as she sobbed into his shoulder.

Chapter Eighteen

⁓⁕⁓

As the evening descended upon Nathaniel's humble abode, the atmosphere grew heavy with tension, each passing moment laden with the weight of uncertainty and fear. Kitty watched Nathaniel's every move, her heart pounding with a mixture of apprehension and gratitude.

"Nathaniel," she began tentatively, her voice barely above a whisper. "Are you alright? I never meant for you to get involved or hurt. I mean—I didn't even know he was going to find me."

"Who is he, Kitty? What a horrid, dangerous man."

"He—he," she brought her hands up to her eyes and covered them. When she looked up again they were wet with tears. "He's the one who killed my husband. That wretched man did nothing but hurt me at the mill, I had no choice but to—" Her cheeks turned mottled and pink and she looked away to avoid the empathy in Nathaniel's eyes. "I didn't have a choice but to succumb to his advances, we needed the money desperately. If I hadn't done what he said, then we wouldn't have had any more work at the mill. He would have seen to that." Kitty felt a heaviness in her chest that felt like it was crushing her soul.

"Oh, Kitty, that's dreadful." Nathaniel said.

Kitty walked over to her saving grace and helped him into the worn chair. "I will get some water and a cloth." She walked to the kitchen and the tears started to fall. She gripped tightly onto the edge of the table and tried to catch her breath.

"Ma?"

"Oh, Grace, come here."

The young girl walked over to her ma and held on to her tightly.

"I promise I won't let him near us ever again," she said, kissing the top of her daughter's head.

"I think we should stay here, ma. He could follow us otherwise."

Kitty knew her daughter was right. She wanted nothing more to do with Frank Wilson, she hated every fibre of his being and Nathaniel's house was the only place where she felt safe. She would have to talk to Nathan.

"Here," let me wash your wounds for you," she knelt down and patted Nathaniel's cuts with a cloth soaked in water.

Nathan winced and flinched slightly. "Grace is right you know, you are safe here, let me protect you both."

"But he came for us here, he knows where we are now. How do I know he won't come back?"

Nathaniel had a fleeting thought of how to solve the situation and make sure Frank would never find Kitty or Grace again, then changed the subject.

"It's a good thing I came back, wouldn't you agree?"

Kitty nodded, then stood up and walked over to the fire to stoke the flames. "Yes, I don't know what I would have done if you hadn't."

"Don't worry about that now, I'm just glad you're both safe."

Kitty couldn't deny the fire burning inside of her and the feelings she had for Nathaniel. The guilt of feeling this way about another man so soon after Edward dying was pushed to one side just for a moment. "Could Grace and I stay for supper? It feels so inappropriate asking that after what I said to you last night, but it's so cold outside and—"

"Shh, there is no need to justify or explain why. You are welcome here any time."

After calling on young Fred next door and asking him to deliver a message to the ragger's school as to why Nathaniel hadn't returned that day, they all tried to sleep deeply. But after the events of the day, they were all on edge. Flinching at the slightest sound and their heartbeats so loud in the dead of night, they were convinced the entire street could hear.

After a couple of hours restless sleep and tossing and turning, Nathaniel carefully got out of bed. He crept into Kitty and Grace's room to check on them, both appeared to have finally nodded off. He pulled an extra blanket from the shelf and placed it over them.

He walked down the stairs and slipped outside. Nathaniel Westford had a job to do if he was to make sure that the woman and child who had burst unexpectedly into his life were to remain safe.

His steps were guided by the memories of comrades long gone and the promise of justice yet to be served. Each step echoed against the cobblestones, a steady rhythm that matched the pounding of his heart.

As he walked, Nathaniel's thoughts turned to his comrades from the Crimean War, men whose loyalty and courage he trusted above all else. He knew that with their help, he could track down Frank Wilson and ensure that he faced justice for his heinous actions.

It didn't take long for Nathaniel to find his friends, a band of brothers bound by the trials of war and the bonds of camaraderie. With a grim determination, he relayed the details of Frank's crimes and his intent to see him punished for his sins.

The men never slept because the dark triggered their past and in the dead of night they listened intently, their faces set in stone as they pledged their support to Nathaniel's cause. They knew the dangers that lurked in the shadows of Whitechapel, but they also knew that justice must be served, no matter the cost.

"You do understand that this can't get back to me, don't you? I know it's asking a lot from you, but I can't afford for any of what I have asked be attached to my name."

"Nathaniel, please. You don't have to mention that. You saved us from death and we are eternally grateful, aren't we?" Richard looked around the room at his two friends who had been like brothers since returning to the streets of Whitechapel. The scars across his face and neck would be enough to scare anybody away with just a glance and without a word. Nobody wanted to rebel against Richard, they could tell in an instant what he had been through just by looking at him and knew he wasn't a gentleman to fight against.

"Thank you, Richard. I appreciate you, all of you."

"Leave it with us," Sam said. "Your deed will be done and we will report back when there is no trace of him." Sam was the youngest of the group, but strong and fearless. With his blonde hair and blue eyes, he looked the gentlest out of all of them. You could be forgiven for thinking that he would let you win, but not Sam.

When Nathaniel left to head back home, together, the three gentlemen set out into the night without a second thought to hunt Frank down. And when they would find Frank's hiding place, justice would be served.

Nathaniel felt a sense of grim satisfaction wash over him, knowing that soon, Kitty and Grace would not have to worry anymore. That justice would be done for Edward's death and the loss of Peter, and life going forward should be happy and peaceful if Nathaniel got his own way.

Chapter Nineteen

⁂

The friends brought together from troubled times gathered underneath the cloak of night, whilst the streets of Whitechapel whispered tales of deprivation, sorrow and despair. Richard, Sam, and Oscar moved with purpose through the shadows, their footsteps muffled against the cobblestones.

"Maybe we should slow down a bit, we don't want to draw attention to ourselves. Nathaniel made it very clear this had to be done discreetly and with no comeback to him." Richard, the older, wiser, and more muscular of the three men led the way. He looked from side to side, relying on Oscar at the back to keep checking behind them.

Sam instinctively slowed his pace forcing Oscar to take it steady. Richard turned around and was pleased his friends had listened to him.

"Do you think Nathaniel has a new lady?"

"That's none of our business, Oscar, and we shouldn't be asking. As long as Nathaniel and those he wants to protect are safe going forward, that's all that matters."

Oscar rolled his eyes. He was the most mischievous of the three who would have regularly got him and his friends into trouble if it hadn't been for Richard and Sam keeping a watchful eye on him. Although he was the shortest of his friends, he could protect himself if needed using tactics he learned at the age of 18 in the army.

Their search for Frank Wilson led them down winding paths and darkened alleys, where the echoes of their footsteps mingled with the distant sounds of the city. Richard's heart raced with anticipation knowing that he would be helping out a dear friend. Nathaniel's request meant the world to Richard, it showed he could be trusted with something as important as Nathaniel and his friend's and child's life.

As they moved deeper into the heart of Whitechapel, the air grew thick with tension. They could feel Frank's presence getting closer as they headed for the mill that Nathaniel had told them about. The journey would take them two hours and they were warned it was best by foot.

"No omnibuses, no coaches, I want this to be as anonymous as possible," Nathaniel had reiterated over and over again until the three friends agreed to walk. "I will reward you all, you can be sure of that." Each of the three men nodded.

Finally, they came upon a large building with eight rows of windows, each one twenty windows across. The chimneys loomed over them and shadowed each of the worker's houses, leaving darkness and gloom on anything that was in the shadow's path.

With a silent nod, they moved towards the building, their senses heightened and they each crouched down behind the wall, waiting for Frank Wilson to appear. They had been told what he looked like, made all the easier by the gash across his face where Katherine had struck him with the sharp edge of the poker.

They waited for what seemed like hours. Their stomachs rumbled, aching for food and sustenance to see them through their task, but they ignored the grumbling sounds and pressed on.

Frank Wilson left the mill by the back door, the movement caught Oscar's eye. He lifted his head from behind the bush to get a better view. "I see him," he whispered. "I'm pretty sure it's him, he's just leaving now."

Richard and Sam moved slightly and slowly and nodded to each other.

"Okay, I will approach him and ask him for directions, I will delay him. Then, when I think he is relaxed and thinks he's safe, I will signal for you both to follow him," Richard said.

Frank walked along the footpath down the side of the mill. Each and every thought he had was of Katherine and how to get his own way. His fists pumped with adrenaline, then he reached for a cigarette and lit it. He looked all around to make sure no one was following him, which is why he was surprised when the stranger approached him.

"What the?—"

"Sorry, I didn't mean to frighten you. I was just wondering which way it was to Willowbrook, do you know it?"

Frank eyed the man suspiciously. He knew that was where Katherine and her family had lived and he didn't believe in coincidence. "Why do you need to know?"

"Oh—my brother lives there, you might know him?"

"No, sorry, I'm not from there, I just look after the mill so I probably won't have crossed his path. If you keep walking straight ahead though, you should reach the village in about fifteen minutes."

Richard nodded, then turned around and walked in the other direction, he waved at his two friends as he walked back towards them.

"I said, straight on, not that way," Frank shouted. *Imbecile*, he muttered under his breath. He walked a few more footsteps, puffing away on his nicotine and thoroughly enjoying every intoxicating inhalation. Turning his mind back to Katherine, the arm around his neck came as a surprise.

"You have nowhere left to run, Wilson," Richard said, having caught up with Oscar and Sam. "Justice will be served for your crimes."

Frank's eyes darted around, searching for an escape that would never come. With a desperate cry, he lunged forward, but Richard and his comrades were ready. They subdued him quickly, their years of training and experience proving invaluable in the heat of the moment.

"Please, please, don't hurt me, I haven't done anything wrong, I promise."

"No?" Oscar shouted close to Frank's face, splattering phlegm filled spittle across his skin. "This one is for Kitty."

Without another word, a flying punch knocked Frank to the ground, rendering him unconscious.

Wary of their surroundings and the potential number of workers witnessing the event, they were glad it was pitch black.

The three men gathered their strength and lifted Frank to the top of the dry stone wall next to the river. The recently heavy rain fall provided rapids and a rush of white water tumbling over rocks and down a slight incline. Frank's body, when pushed over the wall, fell into the dark, murky water below and Richard, Sam, and Oscar snarled as they watched Frank being carried downstream.

They each slapped their thighs, brushing any remnants of Frank Wilson from their hands, then walked back towards Whitechapel in the dead of night.

Chapter Twenty

The morning sun cast a gentle glow over the streets of Whitechapel as Nathaniel Westford awaited news from his comrades. His heart was heavy with anticipation, knowing that the fate of Kitty and Grace rested in their hands. As he paced the worn floorboards of his humble home, his thoughts turned to the events of the previous night and, the sense of justice that had guided their actions.

Nathaniel expected word this morning that the requested deed had been done. He didn't want Kitty to know what he had asked of his old friends. He thought the attention and protection might be too much for her to consider and, his tenderness and empathy too much too soon. He crept upstairs and checked she was still sleeping with Grace. He closed the door gently so as not to disturb them, then went back downstairs to make some tea.

It wasn't long before a knock sounded at the door, and Nathaniel hurried to answer it. Standing on the threshold were Sam, Richard, and Oscar, their expressions grim but determined and satisfied.

"Nathaniel," Richard began, his voice tinged with urgency. "We have news."

Nathaniel's heart skipped a beat as he ushered them inside, eager to hear their report. When the three gentlemen were inside, he looked up and down the street to check no one was watching, then closed the door.

"We found him," Sam continued, his voice steady despite the gravity of their words. "Frank Wilson is no longer a threat."

Relief flooded through Nathaniel as he listened to their account of the events that had transpired. "Did anyone see you?"

"Not that we know of," Richard responded. "It was dark and we believe all the workers had left. There was no one else around."

Nathaniel smiled with relief and shook each of his friend's hands. "I can't thank you enough. What you have done has—" He worded his next sentence carefully. Nathaniel didn't want his true feelings for Kitty made known. He was a private man with a reputation as a headmaster to uphold. "—I will be forever grateful."

Each of the men looked at Nathaniel and nodded, choosing to not say another word about the events of the night before. The less it was discussed, the less chance of them slipping up in conversation.

As they spoke, Kitty stood silently behind the doorway, her eyes wide with disbelief. She had overheard their conversation, unable to tear herself away from the truth of Nathaniel's actions. She had never imagined that anyone could be so kind, so selfless in their efforts to protect her and her daughter.

Kitty heard the men say their farewells and tiptoed up the stairs as quickly as possible. She leaned against the wall out of sight, and heard the front door close. She slipped quietly back into her bedroom.

Nathaniel knocked gently and opened the door - to his surprise Kitty was sitting on the side of the bed. She looked at him and he knew instantly that she had heard.

"Nathaniel," she whispered, "Is it true? Did you—dispose of him?"

Nathaniel turned to face her, his expression softening at the sight of her tear-stained cheeks. He presumed by the softness of her voice that any anger was absent and he was safe to tell her the truth.

He replied gently. "Frank Wilson has been dealt with, that's all you need to know. You and Grace are safe now."

Overwhelmed with emotion, Katherine leant forward and wrapped her arms around him, her gratitude overflowing.

"Thank you," she murmured, her voice choking with tears. "Thank you for everything."

Nathaniel held her close, the weight of her gratitude warming his soul. In that moment, he knew that he had done the right thing, that his actions had brought light into the darkness of their lives.

Chapter Twenty-One

Grace skipped ahead, her laughter ringing out like a melody on a sweet, summer's day. She turned back to her ma and Nathaniel, her eyes shining with excitement.

"Ma, are you and Mr Westford getting married?" she chirped, tugging at her sleeves.

Kitty blushed furiously at her daughter's boldness, shooting Nathaniel an apologetic glance. But Nathaniel merely chuckled, his eyes twinkling with amusement.

"I suppose Grace has a point, Kitty," he said with a playful grin. "We can't deny the truth forever. Or is it far too soon?"

Kitty's heart fluttered at his words, her mind awash with conflicting emotions. It had only been six months since Edward's death, and the wound was still fresh in her heart. But with each passing day, Nathaniel had become a beacon of light in her darkness, a source of strength and comfort she never knew she needed. It was Edward who had told her you should live for every day because you don't know what's around the corner.

"I—I don't know, Nathaniel," she stammered, her voice barely above a whisper. "It all feels so complicated."

Nathaniel reached out and took her hand in his, his touch sending shivers down her spine.

"I understand," he murmured, his voice gentle and reassuring. "But sometimes, the heart knows what it wants, even when the mind protests."

Kitty's eyes met his. She knew that she should resist, that she should mourn Edward's memory and honour their vows. But with Nathaniel by her side, she couldn't help but feel alive in a way she hadn't in months.

As they continued their stroll through the bustling streets of Whitechapel, the conversation turned to the future and what it would mean for their families. "I want to give us all a better life, Kitty. You and Grace in particular. I know what it's like to lose your loved one and be left with a child. It's difficult and tiring and you never know what to do for the best. You go day by day hoping you are bringing your child up the way your beau would have wanted."

Kitty looked at Nathaniel as he spoke and noticed his eyes gloss over, wet with the start of tears. She squeezed his hand gently. "I suppose I'm just battling with whether it's the right thing for me to do. I have feelings for you, but am I supposed to so soon after Edward?" She looked up to the sky searching for the right words. "I just can't shake the nagging sense of guilt that is gnawing at my soul. Edward's memory still looms large in my mind and is a constant reminder of the life I shared with him and the promises we made to each other" .

Nathaniel stopped walking and turned to face Katherine. He took hold of both Kitty's hands in his and held them in front of him.

Kitty tried to avoid his gaze, knowing that if she looked into the depths of his eyes she would never look back. "I don't know if I can do this, Nathaniel," she confessed, her voice tinged with sadness. "Edward was my husband, my soulmate. How can I just—move on?"

Nathaniel's expression softened, his eyes filled with understanding.

"I'm not asking you to forget him," he said gently. "But I believe that love has a way of healing even the deepest wounds. And if you'll let me, I'll stand by your side every step of the way."

Kitty's heart swelled at his words, her doubts fading away in the warmth of his embrace. She knew that the road ahead would be long and difficult, but with Nathaniel by her side, she felt ready to face whatever challenges came their way.

Kitty embraced the promise of a new beginning and felt her heart being held by his. Their hearts intertwined, and they held each other tightly as they imagined building their future full of hope and possibility for them and their children.

Chapter Twenty-Two

Twelve months later.

The dim light of the oil lamp flickered gently in the corner of the room as Kitty clutched the bed sheets tightly, her face contorted with pain. The time had come for her to bring new life into the world, yet with each contraction, she felt the weight of fear pressing down upon her. She wished Peter had been in her life, she felt the weight of her sorrow over Edward's death, and she desperately wanted this child to live but deep down, she had a feeling, which had worried her for weeks.

"I'm sorry, Nathaniel, I'm in so much pain."

"Please my love, do not worry, the doctor is doing his best."

"I know, but I can't—I can't breathe. What if the child isn't born alive?" She lifted her head off the pillow, gritted her teeth, and screamed from the back of her throat.

The room was enveloped in a hushed tension, the air heavy with anticipation as Kitty laboured to bring new life into the world. Nathaniel stood by her side, his hands clasped tightly in hers, his heart pounding with a mixture of fear and excitement.

With each contraction her body convulsed in pain, her breaths coming in ragged gasps as she fought to push through the agony. Nathaniel's voice echoed in the stillness, his words a steady stream of encouragement and reassurance.

"You're doing just fine," he murmured, his voice filled with unwavering support. He tenderly wiped his hand across his wife's forehead and stroked her hair. "Just keep breathing, my love. We're in this together."

Kitty nodded through gritted teeth, her eyes squeezed shut as she summoned every ounce of strength within her. She could feel the weight of their child pressing down upon her, the intensity of the moment threatening to overwhelm her senses.

"Kitty, listen to me." The doctor lifted his head and looked at the mother in labour. "I need you to push one more time, and that will be the last of it, I promise."

Kitty gazed back at the doctor, his blood-stained hands unnoticeable. She witnessed uncertainty in his face and sorrow behind his eyes. Her heart started beating faster as she longed to give birth to another living child, but something was telling her it wasn't meant to be. She held her breath not wanting to push and face the grief and sorrow that would surely follow.

Then, in a burst of raw emotion, the room erupted in a cacophony of cries and shouts as the expectant mother gave one final push.

Nathaniel's grip tightened on her hand, his heart racing as he watched in awe as their child emerged into the world. But instead of a wriggling bundle of life, their precious gift from above making her first cries, there lay a child - so still.

Tears welled in Kitty's eyes as she reached out to cradle their newborn in her arms, her heart overflowing with a love so pure and profound she wanted it to take her breath away, but she already knew that wasn't going to happen.

Instead, both Kitty and Nathaniel leaned in close, their eyes glistening and hearts heavy like rocks with the weight of heartache and grief.

"It's a girl," he whispered, his voice choked with emotion. "But why, Kitty? Why isn't she breathing?"

"I'm so sorry, Mr Westford. The child was—your dear daughter hasn't made it." The doctor closed his eyes and bowed his head.

Kitty nodded, her voice barely above a whisper as she pressed a tender kiss to their daughter's forehead.

"Our daughter," she murmured. "Our precious daughter."

As they held their daughter close, they wondered how they would get through the following minutes, days, months. Their hearts were broken.

They had faced many trials together during their companionship, but nothing could have prepared them for the overwhelming emotions that accompanied what had just happened.

Kitty's heart sank as she looked into Nathaniel's eyes, her worst fears had been confirmed in an instant. Their child, their precious little one, had slipped away before ever taking her first breath.

Tears welled in her eyes as she reached out to Nathaniel, her heart breaking with grief. They had dreamt of a future filled with laughter and love, yet now, the cruel hand of fate had shattered their hopes.

As the weight of their loss settled over them, Grace stood frozen in the doorway, her eyes wide with shock and disbelief. She wanted nothing more than to rush to her mother's side, to offer comfort and solace in her time of need. But in that moment, she felt powerless to do anything but watch as her family grieved the loss of their child.

In the darkness of the room, amidst the stifling silence, Kitty and Nathaniel clung to each other, their hearts intertwined in a bond that could never be broken. And as they mourned the loss of their child, they found solace in the knowledge that they would always have each other, no matter what trials lay ahead.

Chapter Twenty-Three

As the days stretched into weeks following the death of her sister, Grace remained a constant presence in her ma and Nathaniel's lives, her unwavering support a source of solace amidst the storm of grief that threatened to engulf them. With each passing day, she tended to their needs with gentle care, offering a shoulder to lean on and a listening ear for their sorrowful hearts.

One evening, as the soft glow of twilight bathed the room in a warm embrace, Grace sat by her ma's side, their hands intertwined in a silent gesture of solidarity. Kitty, her eyes reflecting the flickering flames of the hearth, seemed lost in thought, her gaze distant as she wrestled with the weight of her sorrow.

"Ma," Grace began softly, breaking the silence that hung heavy in the air. "I know this pain feels unbearable, but you're not alone. We're in this together."

Kitty turned to her daughter, her eyes brimming with unshed tears. "Oh, Grace," she whispered, her voice choked with emotion. "I miss her so much. I keep thinking about all the things we'll never get to do together, all the memories we'll never get to make."

Grace's heart ached at the sound of her ma's grief, her own tears threatening to spill over as she reached out to wrap Kitty in a comforting embrace. "I miss her too, ma. I know that sounds strange because she isn't here and she has never been alive, but I miss our future together as sisters. But we'll carry her memory in our hearts forever. She'll always be a part of us."

Together, mother and daughter sat in quiet communion, their shared sorrow mingling with the warmth of their love as they sought solace in each other's arms. Amidst the pain and the longing, they found strength in their bond, a bond that would endure even in the face of life's greatest trials.

As mother and daughter sat by the fire wrapped in grief, Nathaniel joined them, his weary eyes reflecting the toll that grief had taken on his spirit. Yet, despite the heaviness that weighed upon him, there was a flicker of determination in his gaze, a silent vow to weather the storm alongside his beloved family.

"We'll get through this," he murmured, his voice a steady anchor in the sea of sorrow. "As long as we have each other, we can face whatever challenges come our way."

"I hope so, Nathaniel, I really hope so."

Archie stood in the doorway, he didn't know what to say. He just looked on until he felt so out of his depth and wrapped in loneliness, he shuffled forward quietly then went to sit on his pa's knee.

"Oh, Archie, you are never too old for this," Nathaniel said, kissing the top of his son's forehead.

Kitty looked on and was in awe of how much Nathaniel cared for his son. She accepted it was hard for him to spend a lot of time with Archie. Most of the attention came from Nathaniel as a teacher, but she realised that in the midst of family tragedy, Nathaniel would be there for all of them whatever crossed their path as a family.

Chapter Twenty-Four

Days turned into months, and Nathaniel struggled with the loss his family had suffered. He turned up at the ragger's school, giving his all as a headmaster making sure the children continued to learn. But others noticed that he spent weeks and months vacant behind the eyes.

"Mr Westford," Mrs Mason said as she stepped out of the classroom, shutting the door quietly behind her.

"Yes, Mrs Mason? What is it? Are the children playing up?"

"No, not at all," she hesitated. Would what she was about to say destroy the relationship with Nathaniel Westford, which she had enjoyed as a teacher and friend? "Can I just say something, if you don't mind?"

"What is it? It sounds serious to me the way you are hesitating."

"I've noticed, you're not really here."

"Of course I am, I turn up every day," his sharpness of tone took Mrs Mason back a little.

"No one is doubting your physical presence, it's just that—and I know what you have been through is tragic. But, you are not here in the school with the enthusiasm and grace you had before—" Mrs Mason gazed towards the floor, she instantly regretted saying anything.

"Do you mean before our child died at birth?"

Mrs Mason breathed out heavily. "Yes, that is what I mean, but I was too afraid to bring the subject up. You know how I value our friendship."

Nathaniel gently placed his hand on her shoulder. "I know, thank you. I'm just finding it so hard."

"I know you are, and you can talk to me anytime. But for the children's sake and yours, please do something about it, you can't continue like this." Mrs Mason looked both ways before gently touching Nathaniel on his forearm and returning to the classroom.

As Nathaniel wandered home through the bustling streets of Whitechapel, the conversation with Mrs Mason weighed heavily on his mind. Losing their daughter had left a void in his heart, a pain that seemed to echo through the very depths of his soul. Lost in his own grief, he barely noticed the figure that approached him until a familiar voice called out his name.

"Nathaniel? Is that really you?"

Startled, Nathaniel turned to see an old friend standing before him, his face worn and haggard from years of grief and despair. It was William, a man whom Nathaniel had known since childhood, yet who now seemed like a shadow of his former self.

"William," Nathaniel exclaimed, his voice tinged with surprise and concern. "I haven't seen you in years. How have you been?"

William's eyes bore into Nathaniel's, their depths filled with a sorrow that seemed to stretch beyond the horizon. Nathaniel couldn't help but notice how William looked, his once vibrant spirit now dulled by the weight of his grief. His clothes were threadbare, his face weathered and worn, a stark contrast to the lively friend Nathaniel remembered from their youth.

"Not well, I'm afraid," William replied, his voice barely above a whisper.

"I'm sorry to hear that, where are you living now?"

"Oh, you know, bed to bed, the mites leave me ill, and I'm always hungry." William leant on the weathered stick, occasionally wobbling and then re-gaining his balance. The rims around his eyes were bright red, his eyes sunken into his head.

Nathaniel noticed the wrinkles of worry and grief were so deep, he wondered how long it had been since his friend had smiled.

"I don't like to ask, William, but have you—?"

"Not a chance I have another woman, no one would come near me. All I talk about is how I miss Betty and Rowena. God bless their souls, I long to join them."

Nathaniel's heart clenched at the sight of his friend's despair, the weight of his words sinking like a stone in the pit of his stomach. "I'm so sorry, William," he murmured, his voice heavy with emotion. "I can't imagine what you must have been through."

A heavy silence fell between them, punctuated only by the distant sounds of the city. In that moment, Nathaniel felt a surge of empathy for his friend, a deep-seated understanding of the grief and despair that had consumed him.

"I tried to move on, Nathaniel," William continued, his voice choked with emotion. "But every day feels like a struggle, a battle against the memories that haunt me. I miss them so much, and I don't know how to go on without them. I pray for God to take me, but for some reason he makes me wake up every day and face another twenty-four hours without them." William's shoulders sank even more into the ground and he shook his head.

Nathaniel reached out a hand, placing it gently on William's shoulder. "I know it may not seem like it now, but you're not alone, my friend," he said, his voice filled with conviction. "We may have lost our loved ones, but we still have each other. And together, we can find a way to move forward."

For a moment, Nathaniel and William stood there, their hearts heavy with grief yet bound by a shared sense of loss. In that moment, Nathaniel felt a flicker of hope ignite within him, a spark of light that seemed to pierce through the darkness of his despair.

"Here," Nathaniel said, "it's all I have on me, but take this." Nathaniel reached into his deep pocket and handed over the loose coins. "It's not much but it may help you through the next few days."

William held his hand out, then looked up at his old friend, his eyes showing a glimmer of brightness at the thought of not going hungry for a few days. "I—"

"You don't have to say anything, William."

As they parted ways, Nathaniel couldn't shake the feeling that perhaps, in reaching out to help his friend, he had also taken a small step towards healing his own heart. And as he made his way back home to Kitty, Grace, and Archie, he vowed to cherish every moment they shared together, knowing that life was too precious to be wasted on grief and regret.

Chapter Twenty-Five

As the evening sun dipped below the horizon, casting long shadows across the Westford household, Grace and Archie sat in the cozy living room, a flickering fire casting a warm glow over the room. The events of the past few months weighed heavily on their minds, the sight of their parents struggling with grief leaving an indelible mark on their hearts.

Grace fidgeted with the hem of her dress, her brow furrowed in deep thought. "Archie," she began, her voice hesitant. "Do you ever feel like we should be doing more to help?"

Archie glanced up from the book he had been reading, his eyes meeting Grace's with a mix of curiosity and concern. "What do you mean, Grace?"

"I mean, seeing ma and Nathaniel upset and sad every day, it just made me realise how we can cheer them up."

Grace, with a solemn look on her face, eyed the heaviness that had seemed to hang over their parents lately. Archie, sitting beside her with a furrowed brow, echoed her concern.

"I know, It's like they're carrying the weight of the world on their shoulders," Archie replied, his voice tinged with worry.

Grace nodded, her gaze fixed on the flickering flames in the hearth. "It's all on account of the baby we lost, isn't it? Ma hasn't been the same since, and your pa, well, he tries to put on a brave face, but you can see the sorrow in his eyes."

Archie let out a small sigh. "It's a terrible thing for them to go through."

Grace's lips tightened, a mix of sadness and determination in her expression. "True enough. But maybe we can help lift their spirits, eh? Offer them a bit of comfort with our words or lend a hand with the chores."

Archie's eyes lit up at the idea. "Oh, Grace, that's a grand notion! A little kindness might just make their burden a bit easier to bear, even if only for a short while."

Grace grinned back at him. "Right you are, Archie, I'm sure they would like us to help."

"We can each do our part, Grace, let's help them together."

Encouraged by Archie's support, Grace felt a renewed sense of purpose stirring within her. "I want to do more, Archie," she declared, her voice filled with conviction. "I want to help as many people as I can, in any way I can."

Archie smiled, tentatively reaching out to take Grace's hand in his own. "And I'll be there for you, you're like my best friend, more so than a sister."

Grace smiled at Archie as they shared a silent vow, their hearts united in a shared desire to help their parents feel better. And they knew that no matter what challenges lay ahead, as long as they had each other, they could overcome anything.

Chapter Twenty-Six

Six years later.

Seven years had passed since Nathaniel and Kitty's love had blossomed amidst the cobblestone streets of Whitechapel and six years since they lost their newborn daughter. The streets had changed, its scars from years of hardship still visible, yet there was a sense of hope in the air.

Grace was growing into a young woman of charm and determination, her fiery spirit undimmed by the trials she had faced in her short life. Meanwhile, and watching her from a distance every day, Archie, the childhood friend who had grown up alongside Grace, harboured a secret admiration for her that burned like a flame in his heart. He watched her from afar, captivated by her beauty and her unwavering dedication to helping others.

But while Archie's feelings for Grace were clear, her heart was torn between her love for him and her burning desire to pursue her dreams of becoming a nurse in London.

One evening, as the sun dipped below the horizon and the stars began to twinkle in the night sky, Archie found himself walking alongside Grace through the streets of Whitechapel. His heart pounded with nervous anticipation as he struggled to find the words to express his feelings.

"Grace, I thought we could go to the park, it's such a beautiful evening," he began tentatively, his voice barely above a whisper. "There's something I need to tell you."

Grace turned to him, her eyes alight with curiosity. "What is it, Archie?" she asked, her voice soft and gentle.

Archie took a deep breath, gathering his courage before speaking. "I've admired you for as long as I can remember, Grace," he confessed, his heart racing with every word. "You're the most incredible person I've ever known, and—I'm in love with you."

Grace's heart skipped a beat at his words, her mind swirling with conflicting emotions. She cared deeply for Archie, of that there was no doubt, but her dreams of becoming a nurse tugged at her heartstrings, pulling her towards a future that seemed worlds away from the life she knew.

The couple crossed the street, Archie's hand reaching for Grace's as he guided her to the green grass of Victoria Park.

"Look, there's a bench," he said.

Grace took a deep breath. She wasn't ready for this conversation. The young woman had known for a while that Archie had admired her. She could tell by the way he looked at her, helped her with tasks without being asked. The way he had been by her side during their school days was admirable. But now, Grace was ready to be independent, with a burning desire to leave home and study.

Grace flattened her dress at the back and sat down on the wooden bench. She looked up to the evening sun wishing Archie hadn't said anything, that they could just continue as friends as if they were brother and sister. She didn't want to hurt his feelings, he had been so good to her. How could she possibly tell him she wasn't ready to marry? She was merely sixteen, with her world in front of her. The desire to do more and be more coming from watching her ma work in the wretched mill.

"I—I don't know what to say, Archie," she stammered, her voice filled with uncertainty. "I care for you deeply, but I have dreams of my own, dreams that I can't ignore."

Archie's heart sank at her words, a pang of disappointment coursing through him. He had hoped that she would reciprocate his feelings, that they could build a future together filled with love and happiness. But now, faced with the reality of her dreams, he knew that their paths might soon diverge.

"Please, Grace," he said softly, his voice tinged with sadness. "I want to spend the rest of my life with you."

"I can't, Archie. I'm so sorry. I knew this was going to happen and was dreading you asking."

"Why?"

"Because you have been so kind to me over the years. When your pa took me and ma in, you accepted me with your open heart and took care of me. You didn't leave my side."

"It was the right thing to do."

"And I would have done the same. I'm just not sure it's turned into love for me like it has for you. I feel guilty saying that, I don't want to hurt your feelings."

"Only I can hurt my own feelings, Grace. Maybe I should have realised that you were too good for me."

Grace turned to face Archie on the bench and reached for his hands. "Please never say that, Archie. Nobody is ever too good for you. You have the softest of hearts and the best of intentions, I know that you will make a good husband to the right woman."

"But Grace, you are the right woman."

"I'm not, Archie, not for you. I consider you a brother, not a lover. It wouldn't feel right."

"Give it time, Grace. Not everybody is in love when they court before they get married. Courting is about getting to know each other and learning whether you are both compatible for marriage."

"I agree, Archie. But I have to feel something too. I want to know if there is a chance of love for us. I don't want to get married just because it is the right thing to do. After seeing what happened to my pa, and losing Peter, it's important to me that I have deep feelings for the man I'm going to marry."

"You don't love me?" Archie's eyebrows furrowed together and his lips parted.

"Archie, please. You are making this so difficult for me. Or course I love you, but not romantically. I don't know. Maybe I'm just too focussed on becoming a nurse that I can't think about marriage. But there is so much for me to do in the world, to help the wounded and help them live life again, marriage is just so far from my mind."

Archie knew that if he pushed Grace now, he might lose her forever. His heart felt heavy, and he wondered how he would cope without Grace by his side. Archie turned to the woman he loved. "I understand," he whispered. "It's not what I want to hear, but I feel your desire to do something more. Maybe—maybe when you are ready, we could—"

"Archie, please don't. Let's just leave this conversation as friends. I don't want to be made to feel guilty or coerced into something I might later regret."

Archie nodded. "Okay, I promise it's the end of the conversation."

Grace beamed and lit up with the weight of marriage being lifted from her soul. "Thank you. Now then, why don't we head back and cook the supper we promised our parents?"

"Sounds like a great idea," he said. Archie stood up after Grace and walked home with her. His heart felt heavy, and he tried his best to hide his solemn look. The last thing he wanted in his life was to push Grace away for good.

Meanwhile, Grace didn't want to admit she had a glimmer of hope for her and Archie. If she had voiced her feelings about finding herself at a crossroads of the heart and soul, torn between the love she felt for Archie and the burning desire to forge her own path in life, she may have been persuaded down the wrong path.

Only time would tell if she would come back to him. But for now, she had no desire to tell him that, and instead, pondered what the future held for her.

Chapter Twenty-Seven

"London? Why London?"

"But, ma, we are almost in London anyway, it isn't that far. I want to be a nurse so badly, it's why I went to school, isn't it, Nathaniel?" Grace looked at Nathaniel with expectant eyes. She silently pleaded with him to be on her side.

"Nathaniel? You knew about this?" Kitty said.

Grace looked back at Nathaniel, his lips were parted and he was hesitant in answering. He winced a little knowing he was going to upset one of the women.

"I wouldn't say I knew about it."

"Nathaniel! You did! I spoke to you so many times at school about becoming a nurse. That is why you and Mrs Mason encouraged me with my arithmetic and English. I thought you supported me, Nathaniel?"

"Well—I—"

"Nathaniel, you sound like you are struggling for words. Are you telling the truth?" Kitty looked at her husband with a hand on her hip.

Nathaniel didn't know where to look, he knew he was going to let one woman down. "It's just that—Grace will make an excellent nurse, I know she will. But I also know you will miss her, I just don't know what to say for the best."

Kitty gave a wry smile, "I love you, Mr Westford, at least you are being honest."

Nathaniel sighed. "I just want what is best for both of you, but I suppose I'm a little disappointed too."

"Why?"

"Because, Kitty, selfishly I had hoped that Grace and Archie would marry one day."

"Did someone mention my name?" Archie bounded into the living room. He walked up to the fire, crouched down, and rubbed his hands. "It may be spring but the air is chilly. Anyway, what were you talking about?"

"I was just saying, Archie, I hoped you and Grace would marry one day."

Archie sighed, " So did I, pa, but she has other plans and—"

"Archie, please don't," Grace said.

Archie looked at Grace and smiled. "I was going to say, Grace, we must honour and respect what you want to do. There is no point in falling out just because you have other ideas than to get married. It is obviously your dream to become a nurse."

"Thank you, Archie."

"It doesn't mean I'm not disappointed though. Perhaps in a few years you will come back to me."

Grace blinked slowly and sighed silently. "I just don't know, and I don't want you to wait for me either."

"Very well, I will find another beau, but she won't be as beautiful as you." Archie stood up having warmed his hands and walked over to Grace. He took her hand and kissed it gently.

"I hope you all still love me," Grace looked at each of them in turn, her eyes meeting theirs and starting to form tears. "I have to do what I have to do, and maybe I will return one day," she said, looking at Archie. But for now, I need to leave and fulfil this fire and passion burning inside of me."

The words hung in the air, the weight of Grace's declaration settling over the room like a heavy fog.

"But Grace, London is so far away," Kitty said, her voice trembling with emotion. She walked up to her daughter and wrapped her arms around her. "And nursing is such a dangerous profession, especially in times like these."

"It may be a little dangerous, ma, but London isn't that far away," her voice steady despite the tremble in her heart. "I can't ignore this calling. I want to make a difference, to help those who are suffering like pa did. I can't just stand by and do nothing."

After a moment of tense silence, Nathaniel spoke, his voice quiet yet firm. "Grace, I won't pretend that I'm not disappointed. I had hoped for a different future for you, one where you would marry Archie and stay close to home. But I can see the fire in your eyes, the passion driving you to pursue this path. And I can't fault you for wanting to help others."

Grace nodded, her eyes shining with gratitude as she looked at Nathaniel. "Thank you, Nathaniel. Your support means everything to me."

Kitty's initial shock began to fade. "You've always had a heart of gold, Grace. And if this is truly what you want, then I will stand by you every step of the way."

Tears welled in Grace's eyes and felt a sense of relief wash over her. Despite the uncertainty of the future, she knew that she had the love and support of her family behind her.

As they sat down to supper, the atmosphere in the house was finally one of acceptance and understanding. Archie watched Grace, whilst he ate his supper, and felt the warm broth and vegetables filling every cell in his body. He knew that she was destined for greatness, no matter where her journey took her. But he also sincerely hoped that his love would not diminish when she was away, and that she would return one day to marry him.

Chapter Twenty-Eight

Grace stood on the doorstep of the family home, a sense of anticipation and apprehension weighing heavily upon her heart. The morning air was cool and crisp, carrying with it the promise of a new beginning, yet also the lingering echoes of farewells and bittersweet goodbyes. She held her carpetbag in one hand, a farewell gift from Nathaniel. She turned around to face her ma, Nathaniel, and Archie, and had a brave and courageous look about her. But deep down, her stomach kept turning over in anticipation of what was to come.

Kitty stood beside Grace, her hands trembling as she clutched her daughter tightly. Tears shimmered in her eyes, threatening to spill over at any moment. "Promise me you'll be careful, Grace," she whispered, her voice choked with emotion. "London can be a dangerous place, especially for a young woman on her own."

Grace nodded, her own eyes shining with unshed tears. "I promise, ma," she replied softly. "I'll be careful, I'll stay safe. And I'll make you proud."

With one last embrace, Kitty reluctantly released her daughter, watching as Grace turned to face Nathaniel, who stood nearby, his expression unreadable.

"Nathaniel," Grace began, her voice trembling slightly. "Thank you for everything. For your kindness, your support. I'll never forget what you've done for us. All those years ago me and ma were lost, hurt and homeless. If it hadn't been for you, who knows where we would be now?"

Nathaniel met her gaze, his eyes reflecting a mixture of pride and sadness. "You're a remarkable young woman, Grace," he said quietly. "And you have a strength and determination that will carry you far in life. London isn't that far away, but will feel like a world away when you're not around. Please know you'll always have a friend in me."

"Bye, Archie." Grace gazed to the ground then lifted her head and locked eyes with him. "I—I—"

"Shh, Grace. It doesn't matter." Archie stepped forward and hesitated. "So long airs and graces, I'm going to hug you." He took Grace in his arms. "I'll miss you," he whispered gently in her ear.

"I'll miss you too, now get off me before I cry. And I have an omnibus to catch," she smiled at him as she spoke to soften the intention behind her words. With a nod of gratitude, Grace turned and made her way down the street, her footsteps echoing against the cobblestones as she headed towards the omnibus. The weight of her decision pressed upon her shoulders, the magnitude of the journey ahead becoming increasingly apparent with each passing moment.

As she boarded the omnibus and settled into her hard seat, Grace felt a wave of uncertainty wash over her. The horses lurched into motion, their rhythmic clatter filling the carriage with a sense of urgency and anticipation. London awaited her, a sprawling metropolis teeming with opportunity and danger in equal measure, but she felt ready for it.

As the omnibus hurtled towards its destination, Grace felt a glimmer of hope, a flicker of determination that refused to be extinguished. For she knew that she was embarking on a journey of self-discovery, a quest to find her place in the world and make a difference in the lives of others.

And as the omnibus made its way forward, collecting an eclectic mix of passengers along the way, Grace couldn't help but wonder what the future held in store for her.

Chapter Twenty-Nine

As Grace stepped into the bustling halls of St Thomas Hospital, her heart swelled with a mix of excitement and nerves. Having felt lonely and isolated away from her family she wondered what she had let herself in for.

She had settled into her dwellings the previous evening and, had gone to bed early. She didn't want to face the fact that she had perhaps made the wrong decision. There was no one around for her to talk to and although she had only been away for one day, she missed the conversations by the fire with her ma. She had sat on her bed, her knees brought up to her chest and her chin gently resting on them.

Eventually, she had pulled the blankets up to her chin and fallen asleep so she didn't have to confront her feelings of loneliness.

She took a deep breath in and looked up at the grandeur of the building and the hustle and bustle of doctors and nurses. The tenacity they showed towards patients only fuelled her ambition. She was finally here, ready to embark on her journey to become a nurse.

In the corridors lined with white-coated doctors and nurses scurrying about their duties, Grace's eyes fell upon a figure that stood out from the rest. He was tall, with striking blue eyes and a commanding presence that demanded her immediate attention. He was unmistakably a doctor, and Grace couldn't help but feel drawn to him.

As if sensing her gaze, the doctor turned, his eyes meeting Grace's with a hint of curiosity. For a moment, time seemed to stand still as they locked eyes.

"Hello," he said."

"Oh, hello, I'm sorry. I didn't mean to startle you, I think I was just a little lost." She pierced her lips together and hoped that her reasoning hadn't sounded too shallow.

"Are you looking for someone? Or perhaps you need to be somewhere?"

"Well, erm, it's my first day and I'm not sure where to go," she said, looking around and tiptoeing to look over the doctor's shoulder.

"Oh, I see. You must be Grace Hartman."

"I am, yes, how do you know?"

"Because I was told you were starting today and I was to watch over you. The sister will help you with your training and studies, but ultimately I am responsible for you."

Grace's heart skipped a beat at the thought of the handsome, caring young man watching over her every move."

"Oh, right," Grace's cheeks flushed pink. "In which case, should I follow you?"

The doctor gave a smile that would never be wiped from Grace's memory. It sent shivers down her spine and all the feelings of loneliness from the night before were wiped clean from her mind. She stood frozen to the spot and stared without blinking.

"Are you alright, Miss Hartman?" The deep voice did nothing to bring her back to the moment, it just sent her deeper into trance with thoughts of working with this handsome man side by side. With his dark brown hair and blue eyes, she had already imagined her wedding day and a big family.

"I said, are you alright, Miss Hartman? Have I said something for you to contemplate?"

"No—erm, no. I was just, erm—"

"Come with me, you don't need to explain. My name is Jeremy Cooper, I'm pleased to meet you." He held out his hand to shake Grace's, but she shied away. Jeremy raised his eyebrows, then continued walking down the corridor.

"Grace Hartman, I'm pleased to meet you too."

"I know your name, remember? I knew you were coming." He laughed a little and his smile appeared to stretch from ear to ear.

Meanwhile, Grace's cheeks and neck flushed pink with embarrassment. "Oh, yes, of course you know my name, how silly of me,"

"Don't be so hard on yourself, it's probably just nerves."

Grace was revelling in the individual attention, which confirmed to her that she had made the right decision to come to London. With a bounce in her step, she didn't think anything could wipe the smile from her face.

But the moment was fleeting, shattered by the harsh reality of Grace's surroundings. She turned around to the sound of someone coughing. Grace saw the woman behind her dressed in a grey, floor-length, long-sleeved dress and a white cap.

"Ah, Sister Atkinson, this is Grace Hartman, she is new here today."

"Pleased to meet you, sister."

Sister Atkinson ignored the pleasantries and spoke directly to Dr Cooper. "Doctor, there is a very sick patient who has just arrived, would you care to take a look at him?"

"I will come now." Jeremy Cooper turned on his heels and beckoned Grace to follow with his forefinger.

"You won't be required, Miss Hartman," the sister said in a stern and unwelcoming manner. Go straight to the ward and see what you can help with there."

Dr Cooper shrugged his shoulders behind the sister's back and followed her down the sparse, wooden-floored corridor.

Grace stood frozen to the spot wondering what she had said to upset the sister so quickly.

"Ignore her, she can be harsh sometimes. But believe it or not, she's good at what she does and wants to see you succeed. I'm Emma by the way, I've been here a while so will show you what to do." The blonde-haired nurse had snuck up on Grace without her noticing.

Grace smiled and started to relax a little. "Oh thank you, I'm pleased to meet you. I'm nervous enough as it is without comments like that from Sister Atkinson."

"Like I say, don't let her upset you. Now, let's get you a uniform and you can help, what do you say?"

Grace nodded ambitiously and followed the nurse down the bustling corridors of St Thomas Hospital, her heart filled with a newfound sense of purpose. Despite the cold welcome from the sister, she refused to let anyone diminish her dreams. For Grace knew that she was destined for greatness, and nothing would stand in her way.

CHAPTER THIRTY

As the evening sun dipped below the horizon, casting a warm glow over Nathaniel's and Kitty's home, they sat down to supper, their hearts light and spirits high. The table was set with simple fare, but their laughter filled the room as they shared stories and exchanged fond glances.

"I'm happy, but I miss her, Nathaniel. I hope she comes to visit us soon."

Nathaniel's hand reached across the table for his wife's. "I'm sure she will, my love, and I know she will be missing you too. But life couldn't be better could it?"

"No, it couldn't. I think back to that night when you offered us shelter, and often wonder what would have happened if you hadn't come along. I would probably have been forced back into the mill with Frank Wilson."

"Thank goodness he has gone, I dread to think what would have happened if my friends hadn't dealt with the matter."

"How long has it been since you saw them? It must be a while."

"Come," he said, beckoning her over to sit by the fire. It was a cold winter's night and Nathaniel poked the fire to spark more flame. He passed Kitty a blanket and put it over her.

"Thank you," she whispered. What would I do without you?"

"I don't know, marry some rich man?"

"I don't need riches, just love."

"And that you have, my love."

"Will you see them soon? Your friends?"

"I doubt it. That night seems to have—separated us. I didn't want it to, that wasn't the intention. But I think they were so fearful of saying something that might get them into trouble, we all just drifted apart."

"That's a shame."

"Perhaps, but I also know if I needed them, they would be there."

For a fleeting moment, it seemed as though the shadows of the past had been banished, replaced by a sense of peace and contentment. Nathaniel couldn't remember the last time he had felt so happy, so at ease with the world.

"I love you, Nathaniel."

"I love you—"

Suddenly, as they basked in each other's company, a sharp knock at the door shattered their tranquillity. Nathaniel exchanged a puzzled glance with his wife, his heart pounding with a sense of foreboding.

Kitty said nothing, she just shook her head and frowned.

With a heavy sigh, Nathaniel rose from the table and made his way to the door, his footsteps echoing in the silence of the room. He hesitated for a moment, a sense of unease gnawing at him as he reached for the handle.

As the door swung open, Nathaniel was met with the stern faces of two uniformed policemen, their expressions grave and unreadable.

"Mr Westford?" one of the constables said, his voice clipped and authoritative. "We need to speak with you regarding a matter of great urgency."

Nathaniel felt an icy knot form in the pit of his stomach as he stepped aside to allow the policemen entry. Kitty watched on with growing concern, her eyes wide with apprehension as she joined Nathaniel in the doorway.

"What is this about?" Nathaniel asked, his voice betraying his fear. "What urgency could possibly warrant a visit from the Metropolitan Police?"

The constables exchanged a glance before one of them spoke, his tone sombre and grave. "We have reason to believe that your past may have caught up with you, Mr Westford," he said, his words heavy with implication. "There are allegations of wrongdoing, of a crime committed a while ago. We need you to come with us to answer some questions."

Nathaniel's heart sank as the weight of their words settled over him like a shroud. His past, long buried and forgotten, had resurfaced to threaten everything he held dear. And as he glanced at Kitty, her eyes filled with fear and uncertainty, he knew that their peaceful existence was about to be shattered once more.

Chapter Thirty-One

The dimly lit interrogation room was suffused with an air of tension as Nathaniel sat stiffly in his chair, his hands folded tightly in his lap. Across from him, two stern-faced detectives regarded him with a mixture of suspicion and scrutiny, their eyes boring into his with unwavering intensity.

"Mr Westford," one of the detectives began, his voice low and authoritative. "We'll get straight to the point. We have reason to believe that you were involved in the death of a man by the name of Frank Wilson. Care to explain yourself?"

Nathaniel took a deep breath, his mind racing as he searched for the right words. He sat up straight in his chair and his eyes blazed with confidence. He knew he had to convince the two authoritative gentlemen sitting in front of him that he was innocent, or his entire future would crumble. "I can assure you, gentlemen, I had nothing to do with Mr Wilson's demise," he replied, his voice steady despite the unease churning in his gut.

The detectives exchanged a knowing glance before one of them spoke again, his tone laced with scepticism. "That's an interesting answer, Mr Westford. At least you didn't deny who he was."

The twitch in Nathaniel's lips was tiny, but it felt prevalent in the still, chilling room. He couldn't lie. "I do know him, why would I lie about that?"

"How?" the detective with chestnut hair and groomed moustache asked.

"My wife was having problems with him and she confided in me." Nathaniel's heart raced at the thought of his wife being in danger, his palms began to sweat but he daren't risk rubbing them.

"What sort of trouble? The kind of problem that you would like to fix?"

"No, I'm not that kind of person. I am a headmaster at the ragger's school in Whitechapel. I teach children for a living to have respect and manners for other human beings. Why would I do something that I would never teach the children?"

Detective Simpson rubbed his chin. "That's not what we've heard, Mr Westford. Witnesses have come forward, claiming to have seen you in the vicinity of the crime scene on the night in question. Care to explain why?"

Nathaniel's mind raced through his library of memories until he found what he needed. His three comrades definitely said to him that no one saw them. "Where did it happen? Because I can assure you that I've never been within two feet of Mr Wilson. I wouldn't want to go near him."

"Are you sure about that? I mean, if I knew someone had hurt my wife, I'd want to sort him out." Simpson looked at his partner, Lafferty. "Ain't that right, Detective Lafferty? You'd do it as well wouldn't you?" He guffawed.

"Oh yes, I'd definitely want to have done with him," he snarled.

"This is ridiculous. I wouldn't do anything like that, of that you can be sure."

The detectives regarded him with a mixture of disbelief and suspicion, their eyes narrowing as they scrutinised his every word. "But Mr Wilson was found dead in the Thames estuary, how did he get there?"

"Look, I have no idea." Nathaniel desperately wanted to rest his head in his hands and run through his hair, but he knew if he changed his posture, he'd be behind bars. "I'm not the only one who had a grudge, he upset many people."

The detectives regarded him with a suspicious glance, their expressions unreadable as they exchanged a whispered conversation. After a tense moment of deliberation, Lafferty spoke again, his voice heavy with warning.

"Mr Westford, I suggest you start co-operating with us if you want to avoid a lengthy stay in the clink," he said, his tone dripping with menace. "We have ways of getting to the truth, and if you're hiding something, we will find out."

Nathaniel felt a shiver run down his spine at the detective's words, his mind racing with the implications of what was to come. But as he met the detectives' gaze with a steely resolve, he knew that he would stop at nothing to protect the woman he loved, even if it meant facing the darkest shadows of his past head-on.

With a firm nod, Nathaniel braced himself for the battle that lay ahead, determined to prove his innocence and clear his name once and for all. For he knew that the truth would prevail in the end, no matter the obstacles that stood in his way.

Chapter Thirty-Two

Kitty sat in her chair and bit the wicks of her fingers. *My God, I need you now, Grace, you should be here with your ma, what am I going to do?* She stood up and started pacing the room, her mind whirring with thoughts of a life without Nathaniel, her husband going to jail, or worse, being sent to hang if the detectives found out the truth. But who had come forward?

The front door closed and footsteps were heard in the hallway. The door to the living room opened with a rush. "Kitty, please tell me it's not true? What's happened?" Archie rushed over to her and took her in his arms.

Kitty started crying into her stepson's shoulder. "Oh, Archie, what will I do? I'm not sure what's happened over these past three hours, but it feels like a lifetime since your pa was taken."

"The gossip mongers are out on the street talking about nothing but pa and his murderous ways. What are they talking about? It's not true?"

Katherine had come to a crossroads. Tell the truth and Archie may run from her and his pa for good. Tell lies and he would stay, but then, if he found out the truth he would never forgive them. She battled between right and wrong and silently asked for forgiveness for what was to come. "Of course it's not true. Your pa would never do such a thing."

Archie let out a big sigh, "Oh, that's good. I mean, I didn't doubt him for one minute, but with people talking and making up lies, they make his wrong-doings sound very convincing." Archie took a seat.

"It's not true, believe me, your pa would never do something as criminal as what they are saying."

"Do you know the man they are talking about? Frank Wilson?"

"Yes, Archie, I do. He was the foreman at the mill where I worked and he treated me unkindly. He did things to me that I would rather forget about. That's why Grace and I ran away. I'm still heartbroken over losing Peter, but if we had stayed, I'm convinced he would have worn us into the ground and kept us shackled to the mill. We would have been under his control forever." Kitty brought her fist up to her mouth as her eyes started to water again. "I felt leaving Peter behind was the best thing for him. I don't know now, I just don't know," she said, shaking her head and feeling exasperated. "I thought everything was in the past. Why is it when your life appears to be some kind of normal, things come back to you?"

"I don't know, but what you went through sounds dreadful. We must rescue pa. I don't know how we are going to do it, but we will find a way."

Kitty nodded and smiled meekly at Archie just as there was a knock at the door. Her bottom lip started to quiver and she glared at Archie, her eyes wide.

"Stay there, I will go."

Kitty looked at Archie as he left the room and admired how he had grown into such a fine, young man despite losing his ma at such a young age. She would be forever grateful to him for being with her to protect her from what was to come.

She looked up when a woman walked into the living room behind her stepson.

"I had to let her in, she insisted."

Kitty rolled her eyes at the woman and wondered what gossip the brazen hussy was after.

"Kitty?"

"Yes?" she sighed.

"You'll be pleased to know I'm here to help. I've come to save your husband."

Chapter Thirty-Three

Grace sat in front of the small mirror in her one-room home, her place of safety and one which made her feel comfortable after a long day at the hospital. It was frugal and sparsely furnished, but it was hers and that's all that mattered. She had enough money to pay the rent every week, put food on the table and the rest she put in a battered tin on the shelf above the stove.

The flickering candlelight cast soft shadows across her face as she carefully pinned up her hair. For the first time in what felt like an eternity, she no longer felt lost or adrift. She pondered, as she carefully applied the pins to her dark hair, that the training and friends she had made at St Thomas Hospital had given her a sense of purpose, a direction to her life that she had sorely lacked before.

For years she had missed her pa and brother terribly and having watched her ma abused, she was determined to make her future brighter and heal those who thought they had no chance in life.

She smiled to herself as she thought of Jeremy, the handsome young doctor who had captured her heart. Today, he had asked her to take a walk with him in the park, away from the confines of St. Thomas', and she could hardly contain her delight. He was to call at her home for her and the thought filled her with joy and excitement. She felt blessed to have found someone who wanted to share her journey.

There was a knock at the door, and Grace's heart skipped a beat with anticipation. Having taken one last look in the mirror, she opened the door and saw the shock on Jeremy's face. "It's so good to see you, Jeremy, I've been looking forward to this all day," she smiled sweetly at him. "Come in," she said, hoping they could have a cup of tea before venturing outside. Grace had spent some of her spare pennies on a cake and had cut and laid it out beautifully on one of her finest plates. It had a chip in it and was fading in colour, but the sponge would hide that. Two odd tea cups sat at the side of the plate and the two worn chairs were placed at inviting angles. But something about Jeremy's expression made her heart sink.

"Oh, it's small isn't it?" Jeremy said.

Grace frowned and looked around, trying to decipher what he was saying.

"Your house, I mean," he said in response to her confusion. "I don't think I could imagine living somewhere like this," Jeremy stammered, his voice betraying his unease. His posture and mannerisms betrayed his discomfort, and Grace couldn't help but feel a pang of hurt at his reaction.

Grace felt a lump form in her throat at his words, but she pushed aside her hurt feelings, determined to persevere. She smiled brightly and took Jeremy's arm, ignoring the doubt that lingered in the back of her mind.

"It's not much, but it's home," she said cheerily, her voice steady despite the tremble in her heart. "Shall we go for our walk?" She felt a pang of regret, thinking about the two of them smiling and laughing while enjoying the moist, fluffy sponge cake and tea, but it wasn't meant to be this time.

As they strolled down the street and crossed over to walk through the park, Grace couldn't shake the lingering discomfort from Jeremy's reaction to her home. But she pushed it aside thinking perhaps he was nervous. But that excuse was soon extinguished in her mind as he reached for her hand in his. It felt warm and soft despite his work as a doctor.

"Shall we sit?" he asked.

Grace sat down next to the dashing doctor and felt a sense of déjà vu as she recalled sitting next to Archie as he suggested they court and then marry. She swallowed the hint of emotion and smiled at Jeremy.

"Here, would you like one?" He pulled out a bag of sweet, sugared almonds. "I suppose living in a place like that you have never tried these," he said dismissively.

Grace sincerely hoped that her cheeks weren't turning pink with embarrassment. "Actually, I have, my ma used to buy them for me," she lied. But there was not a chance that she would admit to not being afforded such a luxury. She had more important things to concentrate on whilst she studied and learned.

Jeremy brushed away her response and looked up to the sun. "It's a beautiful day for a walk don't you think, Grace?"

"It is," she said, her faith being restored in his softness and willingness to have a pleasant time with her. "Can I ask, Jeremy, where do you live?"

Jeremy hesitated for a moment before replying, his gaze distant. "I come from a wealthy background," he said finally. "My father is a doctor, and he has high hopes for me. My family's home is in Holly village.

Grace's heart skipped a beat at the mention of Jeremy's family, and she felt a surge of hope that they might accept her despite her humble origins. "I would love to meet them someday," she said, her voice tinged with excitement.

But Jeremy's response was evasive. "Perhaps one day, but let's not tell them where you live."

The words stung her eyes, and she covered her disappointment by swallowing the lump in her throat and smiling sweetly.

"Are your eyes watering, Grace?"

"Er, no, no, it's the sunshine. I'm not used to it. I've been working so hard it's the first time I've stepped outside for a walk in days."

Jeremy nodded. "And I suppose it's not the best place for a walk, my family home has two acres of beautiful manicured lawns and rose bushes with no commoners to ruin the atmosphere."

"I thought you were a caring and loving person, Jeremy. Otherwise, why would you want to become a doctor?"

"Oh, I don't do it by choice, Grace. My father has said if I don't become a doctor he will cut me out of his will. Believe me, his estate means more to me than anything, I couldn't possibly betray what he wants for his only son."

Grace rolled her eyes but continued to make pleasant conversation. Despite his uncharismatic ways and demeaning conversation, she couldn't help but fall for his devilishly good looks and charm, and the hope of wealth in years to come.

"Let's move on shall we, I have somewhere I'd like to take you." Jeremy stood up and took her hand.

Grace put the hurtful comments from the short time they had spent together to the back of her mind and replaced them with the hope that he was going to promise her a future of love, children, and safety.

Chapter Thirty-Four

Audrey Shackleton stood in the centre of the modest living room, her hands firmly planted on her hips, her gaze unwavering as she addressed Kitty and Archie. The atmosphere crackled with tension as Kitty slouched in her chair, weariness etched into the lines of her face, while Archie leaned against the wall, arms folded across his chest, a thoughtful expression on his face.

"I know I wasn't exactly your biggest fan when you first set foot in this 'ouse," Audrey began, her voice cutting through the silence like a knife. "But times are 'ard, and if there's any chance I can 'elp, then I reckon it's worth a shot."

Kitty glanced up at Audrey, a mixture of scepticism and gratitude flickering in her eyes. "We appreciate the offer, Audrey, but I'm not sure what you can do that we haven't already tried," she admitted, her voice tinged with resignation.

Archie nodded in agreement, his brow furrowed in thought. "It's not like we haven't been racking our brains for a solution," he added, his tone laced with frustration.

Audrey let out an exasperated sigh, shooting Kitty and Archie a reproachful look. "You two need to stop being so bleedin' stubborn and listen to reason," she scolded, her voice tinged with frustration. "Me son's been goin' on and on about Mr Westford, says 'e's a decent sort. Reckon if anyone can 'elp, it's me."

Kitty chewed her lip, uncertainty gnawing at her insides. Audrey had never been the most sympathetic of neighbours, but she couldn't deny the sincerity in her offer. Still, the thought of involving Audrey in Nathaniel's predicament left her feeling uneasy.

"I'm not sure, Audrey," Kitty murmured, her gaze flickering to Archie for support. "We don't want to make things worse for Nathaniel. If word gets out that we're meddling ..."

Archie nodded in agreement, his expression grave. "We've got to be careful. We can't risk anyone else getting involved," he cautioned, his voice tinged with concern.

Audrey let out an exasperated sigh, frustration evident in her features. "Oh, for the love of— you two are like a pair of stubborn mules," she muttered, shaking her head in disbelief. "But mark my words, if you don't start thinkin' outside the box, you'll get nowhere."

With a determined glint in her eye, Audrey turned towards the door, her resolve unwavering. "Well, suit yourselves then. But if you change your minds, you know where to find me," she declared, her voice tinged with determination.

"Oh, wait, please."

Audrey smiled to herself before turning around to face Kitty.

"Maybe we should give it a go. I'm not sure what you have planned, but I suppose it might help."

"I knew you'd come round."

Archie rolled his eyes. "Don't be making things worse, Audrey, or I'll never forgive you."

"Listen 'ere lad. I've known you since you were screaming when you came out of your ma, so don't be speakin' to me like that. Audrey returned her gaze to Kitty. "Right then, you comin' or what?"

After considering what would be her only hope, Kitty left the house with Archie and Audrey to make their way to the police station.

Chapter Thirty-Five

The morning dawned bright and promising, with Grace waking up with a contented smile lingering on her face. The memory of her afternoon spent with Jeremy in the park the day before filled her heart with warmth, and she felt a renewed sense of hope for the future. Before she started at St Thomas, she wondered what the future held for her romantically. Would training to be a nurse put any gentleman off desiring her as a wife? She didn't really know, but at least she had Archie to return to if nothing came of her life in London.

As she made her way to St Thomas' Hospital, Grace's steps were light and her spirits high. It seemed as though nothing could dampen her mood, not even the usual hustle and bustle of the busy streets of Victorian London with people getting in her way.

When Grace entered the hospital she could feel her heart racing at the thought of bumping into Jeremy Cooper. After initially feeling less than good enough for the dashing young man, she quickly realised it was probably just his nerves. To try to change his feelings of her slum house, Grace had made sure the place was spotless before he arrived and that she looked immaculate. She wouldn't discuss anything to do with where she lived, instead directing the conversation about her hopes and dreams of one day marrying but still continuing her work as a nurse.

"Grace, you're early today, are you eager to start?"

"I am, Emma. I want to do my very best for these patients and if that means working longer hours and spending most of my time studying, then so be it."

"More like you want to impress someone," Emma said, raising her eyebrows at her friend.

Grace felt herself blush. "No, not at all, my priority and focus is purely the patients."

"I'm only joking, Grace, you don't have to take me so seriously. But I've seen the way you look at each other, just be careful."

"What do you mean, be careful?"

Emma was called urgently by the Sister. "Emma, come now, you can't be talking on these wards. I need you now," Sister Atkinson barked.

"Sorry, I have to go," Emma said, running away from her friend.

Grace frowned. *What is she talking about? Be careful?* She couldn't think what Emma was talking about, so she shook her head and continued towards the nurse's room.

"Help, help!"

Grace turned around to the shouts of a nurse in her long grey dress trying to stop a patient from falling on the floor. She was bent over under the weight of the gentleman, who was bleeding from his head and was semi-conscious. Grace looked around for help, but in the absence of any other doctors or nurses, she ran towards the young woman.

"Here, let me help." Grace grabbed the other side of the patient, but as he passed out and his body went limp, the two nurses had no choice but to place him on the floor. "Quick, get me something to help him."

"I don't know what to do, I'm new."

"Run to the stock room, I need bandages and ammonium carbonate. Quickly then! Don't just stand there staring."

The young nurse suddenly came to her senses and ran down the corridor. She returned quickly, and Grace opened the bottle of smelling salts and held it under the gentleman's nose. There was no movement from the patient, and his head continued to bleed profusely. "Hurry, wrap this around his head, it might stop the bleeding."

"What is going on here?"

Grace looked up to the sound of Jeremy's voice.

"Help, please, he won't stop bleeding."

"What are you doing Nurse Hartman? Why isn't he on a stretcher and why didn't you ask for help? This gentleman is practically dead!"

"I'm sorry, I thought—I thought I was doing the right thing," Grace stammered. "This nurse here—"

"I'll be speaking to you later!"

Grace didn't know where to look and felt the colour in her face rising. Her neck felt like it was burning and her eyes stung with acidic tears.

"Emma, come here quickly, will you help me with this patient?" Jeremy shouted out.

Emma had arrived from nowhere into Grace's vision and helped Jeremy Cooper get the patient onto the stretcher, along with the Sister who had also run to help. The nurse who originally held the bleeding man, stepped back.

Despite Grace's best efforts, the situation took a tragic turn, leaving her feeling helpless and overwhelmed. And to make matters worse, Jeremy had witnessed her mistakes and gave a disapproving gaze that pierced her like a knife.

"Grace, what did you think you were doing?" Jeremy's voice cut through the chaos, his tone laced with disappointment. He looked at Grace after trying to revive the patient to life. His hands were covered in blood and he stood in the middle of the corridor, chastising Grace in front of the other staff.

She couldn't understand his reaction, couldn't comprehend why he would speak to her with such disdain. She thought she was doing the right thing by helping out when she was asked by the nurse.

Jeremy Cooper shook his head and walked off, leaving others below him to clean up the mess and dispose of the body.

Sister Atkinson scorned her with eyes of ice-cold steel.

Within moments, Grace was left alone in the middle of the corridor and she didn't know what to do with herself. She stood frozen to the spot amongst the noises and smells of acrid blood and piercing cries for help.

Later that afternoon, Grace sought solace in the company of her friend Emma Parker, her heart heavy with confusion and hurt. They sat on the chairs in the nurse's room, having taken a few moments away from work.

Emma had guided her friend away from the confines of the hospital wards and their drama when she saw Grace was still upset some three hours after the patient died.

"Emma, I don't understand," she confessed, her voice trembling with emotion. "Why would Jeremy treat me like that? I thought he cared about me." She leaned into her friend's shoulder.

Emma's expression darkened with concern as she hesitated for a moment, choosing her words carefully. "Look, Grace, I know you have been courting Jeremy, but perhaps he isn't the man for you," she cautioned, her voice gentle but firm.

Grace's heart sank at Emma's words, a cold knot forming in the pit of her stomach. "What do you mean, Emma? What aren't you telling me?" she pressed, desperation creeping into her voice. "I think I'm in love with Jeremy, I don't want him to be angry at me. There must be a reason why he shouted at me like that, I just don't understand."

"Look, I think you should—I don't know, perhaps you should ask him why he was like that," Emma said. But before she could say anything else and prevent her friend from heartache, Emma was called away by Sister Atkinson to help with a patient leaving Grace alone with her thoughts. As she finished her shift and made her way home, a sense of unease settled over her like a heavy shroud.

And when she turned the corner away from St. Thomas', the sight that greeted her shattered her world into a million pieces. There stood Jeremy, holding the hand of a nurse that looked familiar from the hospital. When he turned around, the betrayal on his face was plain to see.

As Grace watched them, her heart shattered into fragments, the realisation sinking in like a dagger to the chest. Jeremy was not the man she had thought him to be, and the pain of his betrayal cut deeper than she could have ever imagined.

Chapter Thirty-Six

Nathaniel sat in the dimly lit interrogation room, his hands clenched into fists on the table before him. The air was heavy with tension as the police continued to question him about Frank Wilson's death. He had been behind bars for over twenty-four hours and the police didn't seem to care whether he was hungry, thirsty, or had no sleep. His mind raced, trying to piece together who could possibly be the witness against him. But try as he might, he couldn't shake the nagging feeling of suspicion that gnawed at him.

"I've told you everything I know," Nathaniel insisted, his voice strained with frustration. "I had nothing to do with Wilson's death."

Detective Lafferty exchanged a suspicious glance with Simpson before leaning in closer, his eyes narrowing. "We'll see about that," he muttered, before leaving Nathaniel alone in the room once more.

As the minutes stretched into hours, Nathaniel's anxiety grew, his mind whirling with unanswered questions. Why would they want to incriminate him when he wasn't even there? Someone must have inside information.

Just as Nathaniel was on the brink of despair, the door to the interrogation room swung open.

"Well, it appears someone has come to rescue you, but you're not free to go just yet. They are being questioned in the room next door," Simpson said, pointing his thumb over his shoulder. He moved his hands to his pockets and paced the room slowly and considerately.

"Who is it? Who is here?"

"That's none of your business," Simpson said, moving closer to Nathaniel's face. "All you need to know is that you aren't clear yet, if you ever will be," he snarled.

Nathaniel exhaled loudly and rolled his eyes when Simpson walked out of the room.

"What's going on here?" Audrey demanded, her voice sharp with authority. "Why are you questioning him?"

The officers exchanged uneasy glances, clearly taken aback by Audrey's sudden appearance. But before they could respond, Audrey shook her head sharply and glared at the two detectives in front of her. She waved her hand in front of her face to cut through the cigarette smoke.

"Don't exaggerate Miss Shackleton, I'm sure you've inhaled a few cigarettes in your time."

Lafferty blew smoke rings in the air, took a look at his cigarette then turned his attention back to Audrey. "So tell me, how do you know Mr Westford is here?"

"Well, you know, word gets round, dunnit?"

"Is that right? And where exactly were you when you say you were 'with Nathaniel' on that fateful night?"

"I was WITH him, if you know what I mean."

"And was Mr Westford married at the time?"

Audrey sat up straight in her chair, her hands resting on the top of her bag in her lap. "No? Is that important?"

"I just wondered why Mr Westford would be with you when I've seen his wife."

"He just wanted a bit of company," Audrey said, looking pleased with herself.

"How long were you with him?" Simpson asked, shifting in his seat.

"You wanting to know all the details, detective?"

Simpson cleared his throat as he blushed and shifted again. "No, I just need to hear enough to warrant Mr Westford's release."

"I was with him, I guarantee it."

"What time did he leave your house?"

Audrey had to get this right, she hadn't spoken to Nathaniel so took a considered guess at what time Nathaniel would come up with. "Before midnight, he went back home to Kitty. And he had to get to work the next day at the school, so it wasn't a late one."

"And where's his wife now? Does she know about this?"

Kitty, Archie, and Audrey had agreed it would look less suspicious if they waited out of sight whilst Audrey played her part.

"I don't know where she is? I 'aven't seen her." Audrey's heart beat faster and she hoped the detectives wouldn't be able to hear what she considered a loud thumping of her heart. Her gaze was harsh, and she didn't blink or shift her gaze away from Lafferty. Audrey confidently crossed her arms across her chest and lifted her chin in the air.

"You sure about that?" Simpson said, sighing.

Audrey leaned forward, her arms still folded. "Of course I am, why would I want to see 'er?"

"And how can you be certain it was Mr Westford who visited you that night, Miss Shackleton?" Lafferty said, taking a long drag on his cigarette.

Audrey smiled reassuringly. "I never forget my men," she said quietly.

Lafferty leaned over towards Simpson and whispered, "Go and check Nathaniel's alibi and timings will you? I'll wait here with this one."

Simpson stood up and scraped his chair back making Lafferty wince, Audrey remained still.

"Right, Miss Shackleton, Detective Simpson is going to speak to Mr Westford and if his story matches yours, then he's free to go. Although you mark my words, Miss Shackleton, if either of you are lying or planned this, then you'll be back in here before you know it."

"I'll look forward to it, Detective Lafferty," she said, licking her lips.

Meanwhile, next door, Nathaniel was getting impatient.

"I haven't done anything, I promise. Please, tell me who is here."

Detective Simpson waited until the room was quiet. "A witness in your favour, Mr Westford. A Miss Shackleton."

Nathaniel sat in silence, his eyes darting from left to right, trying to figure out who Miss Shackleton was. *Miss Shackleton, Miss Shackleton, where have I heard that name before?* And, as if all the lights had been turned on to shine a spotlight on the memory he needed, he took a sharp breath in. "Ah, yes, Miss Shackleton, I know the woman well."

"Uh, huh? How's that then?"

Nathaniel still hadn't joined all the dots together that he needed to get himself out of jail. His mouth twisted from side to side, trying to figure out what Audrey Shackleton would have told the detectives.

"Her son is in my school, I teach him. His ma—," he coughed, bringing a fist to his mouth, "—is an interesting character."

"Uh, huh?"

It was obvious that Detective Simpson had no inclination to expand further, hoping to catch Nathaniel out.

Come on, Nathaniel, think, think, what would she have said? He took the one and only chance he had. "She took a liking to me and wouldn't leave me alone."

"What? A man like you getting involved with her?"

"Well, I was a bit upset, you see. Me and Kitty had a bit of an argument."

"Tell me more."

Nathaniel took a deep breath in. "I went to visit Miss Shackleton because Kitty had stormed out of the house. So after a few brandy's, I sort of lost my way and ended up at Miss Shackleton's house."

"I bet you did," Simpson said, raising his eyebrows. "And what did you do at Miss Shackleton's house?"

"Come on, detective, you don't want to know that, do you?"

"Alright then, what time did you leave?"

Nathaniel started to sweat under his collar, he ran his finger under the material trying to shift it away from his skin. "It was er, just before eleven thirty, I had er, work the next day."

"Why are you sweating, Mr Westford?"

"Why am I sweating?" he said, leaning forward. "Are you joking? If Kitty finds out about this then that's her gone for good. She's made me the happiest man alive, and I'm not willing to lose that."

Simpson noticed Nathaniel's eyes watering. "Stay there, Mr Westford." He stood up, scraping the back of his chair again against the cold floor. He shut the door behind him then walked to the next room and knocked on the door.

"Come in?"

"Can I have a word, Detective Lafferty?"

He stood up and stepped outside the room. "Well? What did he say?"

"Well, on the basis that I really don't think there is any way they have both collaborated on this story, I think he's telling the truth."

Lafferty ran a hand across his stubbly chin. "Great, we have got little choice then have we but to let him go?"

"No, we haven't. And to be fair, I don't think the witness accusing him of the murder was entirely genuine, if you want my opinion."

"I tend to agree. I suppose it's not as if anyone is missing Mr Wilson, is it?"

Simpson shook his head.

"Right then, let him go for now." Lafferty walked off after kicking the door making Nathaniel jump.

"Are you alright, Nathaniel?" she asked, her voice gentle.

Nathaniel nodded, unable to find the words to express his gratitude. "I am now," he replied, his voice choking with emotion.

With Audrey's testimony, the police had no choice but to release Nathaniel from custody. As he stepped out of the building, he was met by Kitty's warm embrace, her eyes shining with tears of relief.

"Oh, Nathaniel, I was so worried about you," she whispered, her voice trembling with emotion.

Nathaniel held her tightly, feeling a surge of gratitude for her unwavering support. "I don't know how to thank you both," he murmured, his voice choked with emotion.

Audrey waved off his gratitude with a dismissive gesture. "No need for thanks, Nathaniel. You 'elped my boy when he needed it most. Consider this my way of repaying the favour. "

As they made their way out of the police station, Nathaniel felt a renewed sense of determination coursing through him. He vowed to find out who the witness against him was, determined to clear his name and protect his family at all costs.

None of them noticed the figure standing on the corner across the street. He had one leg crossed over the other, leaning against a brick wall. He exhaled his cigarette smoke into the night, clearly visible against the oil lamps in the still of the night.

Chapter Thirty-Seven

As Grace sat at her desk, the flickering candle casting dancing shadows across the worn parchment before her, she hesitated, the quill poised uncertainty over the blank page. Writing home had been on her mind for days now, a constant tug at her heartstrings urging her to reach out to her mother and Archie. Yet something held her back, a lingering sense of reluctance that gnawed at her conscience.

Was it fear? Fear of burdening them with her troubles, of admitting the cracks that had formed in the facade of her newfound independence? Or perhaps it was pride, that stubborn streak inherited from her mother, refusing to admit defeat even in the face of overwhelming loneliness and doubt.

But as she traced the edge of the parchment with her fingertips, her heart heavy with longing and sorrow, Grace knew that she could no longer ignore the ache in her chest, the yearning for the familiar comforts of home. Jeremy's betrayal weighed heavily on her mind, a wound that festered beneath the surface, poisoning her thoughts and clouding her judgement.

She had tried to push it aside, to bury the hurt deep within her heart and focus on her duties as a nurse. But with each passing day, the pain grew more unbearable, a constant reminder of the fragility of trust and the cruelty of betrayal.

And so, with a resigned sigh, Grace dipped the quill into the inkwell and began to write. The words flowed from her pen, a torrent of emotion and longing spilling forth onto the page as she poured her heart out to those she was closest to.

Dearest Ma and Archie,

I hope this letter finds you both in good health and spirits. How I miss you both terribly! The days here at St. Thomas pass by in a blur of patients and responsibilities, but amidst the hustle and bustle, my thoughts often wander back to the warmth and familiarity of home.

I cannot express how much I long for the comfort of your presence, ma, and the steadiness of Archie's companionship. The hospital is a world away from our humble abode, and though I am making new friends and acquaintances, there is an emptiness in my heart that its bustling corridors cannot fill.

I wish I could tell you that everything is well and good here, but the truth is, something feels amiss. The days are long and tiring, and despite my best efforts to throw myself into my work, there is a lingering sense of unease that I cannot shake.

Don't misunderstand me, ma, I am grateful for the opportunity to train and learn here at St. Thomas. The knowledge and experience I gain each day is invaluable, and I am determined to make the most of this opportunity. But there are moments when the weight of it all feels overwhelming, and I find myself yearning for the simplicity of home.

Archie, I can almost hear your voice in my mind, urging me to be strong and resilient in the face of adversity. You have always been my pillar of strength, my unwavering support, and I draw strength from the memory of your words and encouragement.

I promise to keep you both updated on my progress here at St. Thomas, and I eagerly await the day when I can return home to your loving embrace. Until then, know that you are always in my thoughts and prayers.

Please give my love to Nathaniel.

With all my love,

Grace

As she carefully folded the letter and sealed it with wax, Grace felt a sense of relief wash over her. The weight of her burdens seemed lighter somehow, the act of putting words to paper a cathartic release of pent-up emotions and fears. And though she knew that her troubles were far from over, she took solace in the knowledge that she was not alone, that her family was only a letter away.

Chapter Thirty-Eight

They meant for the home coming to be a celebratory affair. The suspicions of Nathaniel being involved in Wilson's death had been cast aside for the time being, with the unexpected and surprisingly welcome help from Audrey.

When Nathaniel and Kitty returned home under the darkness of the sky, a heavy guilt resting upon them, they had decided to forget about the whole torrid matter again and move on.

But it wasn't meant to be. The dimly lit room felt suffocating as Kitty lay on her bed, her body wracked with fever and her mind clouded with delirium. Nathaniel sat by her side, worry etched into the lines of his weathered face as he watched over her, helpless to ease her suffering.

"Kitty, my dear, can you hear me?" Nathaniel's voice was soft, laced with concern as he reached out to brush a lock of hair away from her clammy forehead.

Kitty stirred, her eyelids fluttering open as she struggled to focus on his face. "Nathaniel?" she whispered hoarsely, her voice barely a whisper. "Is that you?"

"Yes, my love, it's me," Nathaniel replied, his heart aching at the sight of her frailty. "You're burning up. We must get you some help."

She shook her head weakly, a shiver wracking her body as she clutched at the blankets. "No, Nathaniel. I don't need a doctor," she insisted, her voice tinged with stubbornness. "I just need you here with me."

Nathaniel's brow furrowed with concern as he gently pressed a cool cloth to Kitty's forehead. "But, my dear, you're not well. We must find out what's wrong."

Kitty's lips trembled as she struggled to form her words. "It's melancholy, Nathaniel," she murmured, her voice barely audible. "I'm convinced of it. Melancholy, from thinking you might have been taken from me. And Grace isn't here, that doesn't help me."

Nathaniel's heart clenched at her words, a pang of guilt coursing through him. How could he have allowed this to happen? How could he have let his own troubles come between them, to the point where Kitty's health was now in jeopardy? Silently, he vowed to do everything in his power to make things right, to find the witness responsible for dragging his name through the mud and tearing their lives apart.

Meanwhile, Archie watched on with a heavy heart, his own worry mirroring his father's. "Pa," he said softly, pulling Nathaniel aside, "do you think it might be melancholy? Do you think she's right?"

Nathaniel sighed, running a hand through his hair. "Perhaps, son," he replied, his voice heavy with concern. "But we mustn't jump to conclusions. We need to focus on getting her the help she needs."

With a heavy heart, Nathaniel and Archie sat by Kitty's bedside, their minds racing with worry and uncertainty. In the distance, the faint tolling of a bell echoed through the night, a sombre reminder of the fragility of life.

Chapter Thirty-Nine

As the evening sun cast long shadows across the cobbled streets of Whitechapel, Nathaniel Westford found himself standing before the weathered door of his old comrades' gathering place. With a heavy heart and a sense of unease gnawing at his insides, he raised a hand and rapped sharply on the door.

Whilst the police didn't seem to have any further interest in Nathaniel for now, he had a desire to bring an end to the matter once and for all. Someone had been behind his back and he was determined to find out who. With a sick wife at home, he wanted a clear head to be able to help her, it was imperative that he found out who had given his name to the police.

Moments later, the door swung open, revealing Richard, Sam, and Oscar, the three men who had stood by Nathaniel's side through the trials of war and the challenges of civilian life.

"Nathaniel," Richard greeted, his voice gruff but welcoming. "What brings you here at this hour?"

Nathaniel's gaze swept over his old comrades, his heart heavy with the weight of his impending question. "I need to speak with you all," he said, his voice firm. "It's about Frank Wilson's death."

The three men exchanged wary glances, a palpable tension settling over them like a heavy fog. "What about it?" Fred asked cautiously, his brow furrowed with concern.

"I need to know if any of you had a hand in giving my name to the police," Nathaniel stated bluntly, his gaze locking onto each man in turn.

Richard shook his head vehemently. "Not me, Nathaniel. You know I'd never betray you like that."

Sam and Oscar echoed Richard's denial, their expressions a mixture of confusion and concern. But Nathaniel could sense something lingering beneath the surface, a tension simmering just out of reach.

"I'm not accusing any of you," Nathaniel clarified, his voice softening slightly. "But I need to be sure. Frank Wilson's death has put me in a precarious position, and I need to know who I can trust. And now—now Kitty is sick. I need to bring this matter to a close once and for all so I can concentrate on helping her get better."

The three men exchanged uneasy glances, a silent conversation passing between them as they weighed their words carefully. And then, suddenly, Sam's eyes widened with realisation, a look of horror crossing his features.

"Nathaniel," he began hesitantly, his voice barely above a whisper. "I—I think I might know who it was."

Nathaniel's heart clenched at Sam's words, a sinking feeling settling in the pit of his stomach. "Who, Sam? Tell me."

Sam hesitated, his gaze flickering to the ground as he struggled to find the words. "It—it might have been Tommy," he admitted finally, his voice barely audible.

"Tommy?" Nathaniel repeated, his mind racing as he tried to place the name. "Tommy from the trenches?"

Sam nodded, his expression pained. "Yes, Tommy. I—I think I might have let it slip to him one night when we were drinking. I didn't mean to, Nathaniel, I swear."

Nathaniel's heart sank at Sam's confession, a wave of anger and betrayal washing over him. But he pushed aside his emotions, focusing instead on the task at hand.

"Thank you, Sam," he said quietly, his voice tinged with resignation. "I'll deal with this myself."

With a heavy heart, Nathaniel turned and strode out into the night, his mind racing with thoughts of vengeance and justice. Tommy may well have betrayed him, if so, Nathaniel was determined to make him pay for his treachery.

And as he disappeared into the darkness, the echoes of his footsteps fading into the night, Nathaniel knew that his pursuit of justice would lead him down a dangerous path, one from which there would be no turning back.

Chapter Forty

Nathaniel's heart was pounding as he stood before Tommy's rundown dwelling. The surrounding air was heavy with tension as he prepared to confront the man who had potentially destroyed his life. With a deep breath, he knocked on the door, steeling himself for the confrontation ahead.

The door creaked open, and there stood Tommy, wearing a facade of innocence that Nathaniel saw right through. "Nathaniel, old mate! What brings you here after all these years?" His voice sounded jovial, but there was a hint of nervousness beneath the surface.

Ignoring Tommy's attempt at small talk, Nathaniel pushed past him and entered the dimly lit room. "Cut the act. We both know why I'm here," he said, his tone firm and unwavering.

Tommy's expression shifted, his eyes narrowing as he tried to maintain his composure and balance. "I don't know what you're talking about, Nathaniel. I haven't done anything," he protested, but his voice wavered with uncertainty.

Nathaniel fixed him with a steely gaze. "Don't play dumb, Tommy. I know it was you who gave my name to the police."

Tommy's facade crumbled, replaced by a surge of anger. "And what if I did?" he spat, his fists clenched at his sides. "You left me there to die in those trenches, Nathaniel. You abandoned me!"

Nathaniel felt a pang of guilt gnaw at his insides, but he pushed it aside, focusing on the task at hand. "I did what I had to do to save as many lives as possible," he replied, his voice tinged with regret. "It wasn't an easy decision, but it was the right one."

Tommy's face contorted with rage. "Right for you, maybe! Look at me now, Nathaniel. Begging on the streets, with no prospects and no future. All because of you!"

Nathaniel felt a surge of frustration bubbling within him. "You think I wanted this for you, Tommy? You think I don't regret what happened every single day?" he countered, his voice rising with emotion.

Tommy stepped back, fully aware of the emotion in Nathaniel's words. "You shouldn't have left me, you were happy enough to save the others, why leave me?"

"You were so badly injured, Tommy, I didn't know what to do, I didn't even know you had survived!"

"I screamed for you! Of course I was still alive. You just chose the others over me, and it hurt."

"I'm sorry, Tommy, I really am, I just felt like I had no choice."

" I bet you are."

"Look, what do you want from me?" Nathaniel said, looking around the room.

Tommy caught his wandering eyes. "It's not money, I mean, I know it would help. But that's not what I want."

"I'm truly sorry, Tommy. I just don't know what to say then. Let's just leave it shall we? You're alive, I'm alive, our three friends made it—"

Tommy tutted. "Friends? Yeah right!"

Nathaniel shook his head slowly and turned around to walk away. He didn't see Tommy reaching for the poker next to the fire, he only heard the grind of metal as he pulled it off the holder.

"What the—?" Nathaniel lifted his arms to protect his head, then jolted to the side to avoid the iron rod hitting his body. "Tommy! What are you doing?"

Amid the chaos, Nathaniel's determination won, and he managed to overpower Tommy. "Stop! Please! This isn't what you want, it's not worth it. You'll be charged with murder if you knock me down with that."

Tommy swung the poker high above his head again as he broke away from Nathaniel's grip.

"STOP!" Nathaniel shouted at the top of his voice.

Then they both heard banging coming from the room above. "Shur up, I got a bairn trying to sleep in 'ere."

The momentary change of voice and interruption seemed to make Tommy pause. He dropped the poker to the floor and stood doubled over, panting for his breath.

Nathaniel leant over and rested his hands on his knees, all the while looking at Tommy in case he burst into action again. "Stop it, Tommy, just stop."

Tommy slowly closed his eyes and nodded. "Fine, you win, again."

"Please, Tommy, I've got a family, I need to take good care of them, allow me to do that. I've already lost one wife, I don't want to lose another."

Tommy sighed. Exhausted and beaten, and after some discussion, he agreed to go to the police and retract what he said.

"I'll help you in life, Tommy, allow me to do that so you get back on your feet," Nathaniel shouted after Tommy as he was led away to an interrogation room. A short while later Detective Simpson came out to where Nathaniel was waiting.

"You're free from all accusations, Mr Westford, it's been a pleasure meeting you," Simpson said. He held out his hand, but Nathaniel didn't respond and Simpson dropped his arm by his side.

Exhausted but relieved, Nathaniel made his way home, his mind finally at ease now that the threat against him had been dealt with. On arriving home Nathaniel walked through the door, he then climbed the stairs to the bedroom where Kitty was propped up in bed, the blankets lifted high under chin. He gently sat down on the side of the bed and took hold of her hand. "My love, how are you?"

Kitty opened her eyes and looked at her husband with a weak smile.

"I didn't mean to wake you, I'm sorry."

Kitty was so immobilised by grief that she just looked at him.

"I just want to say, it's over Kitty, it's over." He took her in his arms and held her tightly whilst Archie watched from the door, knowing what he had to do next.

Chapter Forty-One

As Grace approached Jeremy, the weight of the letter from home heavy in her hand, her steps faltered. She knew this conversation wouldn't be easy, but she had to ask. She slipped into a side room and read the letter again.

My Dearest Grace,

I hope this letter finds you well, but I must confess that the news I bring is not as I would wish it to be. It pains me deeply to be the bearer of such tidings, especially in written form, but circumstances compel me to convey them to you without delay.

Your beloved ma, Kitty, has fallen ill, and her condition is gravely concerning. I hesitate to burden you with the details, but I fear time is of the essence, and I cannot in good conscience keep you in the dark any longer. It is a heavy weight upon my heart to deliver such news from afar, and I pray you will forgive my shortcomings in this regard.

I have deliberated long and hard over whether to write these words to you, for I do not wish to appear as though I am employing emotional manipulation to compel your return home. However, the urgency of the situation leaves me with no choice but to implore you to consider hastening your journey back to us.

My dear Grace, I cannot bear the thought of you being away from home in such a trying time. Your presence here is sorely needed, not only for your ma's sake, but for your own as well. I know how deeply you cherish your studies and the path you have chosen, but I fear that your ma's condition may not afford us the luxury of time.

Please understand, that it is with a heavy heart and great reluctance that I write these words to you. I would give anything to spare you the pain and worry that I know this news will bring. But I cannot in good conscience keep you from your family when they need you most.

I trust in your strength and resilience, Grace, and I have faith that you will make the right decision for yourself and for your family. Know that you are loved and cherished beyond measure, and that I will be here waiting for you with open arms, whenever you are ready to return.

With all my love and devotion,
Archie

Grace took a deep breath and went to look for Jeremy. She found him with a patient, his smug, confident smile shining through to give the patient hope they would survive.

"Jeremy," she began, her voice steady but devoid of its usual warmth, "I received a letter from home. My ma is gravely ill, and I need to go back to care for her."

Jeremy glanced up from his paperwork, his brow furrowing slightly at the serious tone in Grace's voice. "Is everything alright, Grace?" he asked with apparent concern.

Grace hesitated, her gaze fixed on the floor. "No, everything's not alright," she admitted quietly. "But I need your permission to leave, Jeremy."

Jeremy's expression softened at the sight of Grace's distress. Stepping closer, he placed a gentle hand on her shoulder. "Is there anything I can do to help?"

For a moment, Grace felt a glimmer of hope. Maybe Jeremy would understand, maybe he would give her permission to go home. "Thank you, Jeremy, I just need to attend to ma," she murmured, relief clear in her voice.

But as quickly as it had appeared, the hope vanished. Jeremy's demeanour shifted, his hand falling away from her shoulder. "I'm sorry, Grace, but you can't leave," he said firmly, his tone leaving no room for argument.

Confusion washed over Grace as she tried to process Jeremy's sudden change of heart. "But why, Jeremy?" she asked, her voice tinged with disbelief.

Jeremy sighed, running a hand through his hair in frustration. "There are too many patients, Grace. We need you here," he replied, his tone growing more agitated.

Grace felt a surge of frustration and anger rise within her. "That's not fair, Jeremy," she protested, her voice shaking with emotion. "You can't keep me here against my will."

Jeremy's expression hardened at her defiance. "While you're here, you're under my control and direction, Grace," he retorted sharply, his eyes flashing with irritation.

Tears welled up in Grace's eyes as she struggled to hold back her emotions. "I can't believe this, Jeremy," she whispered, her voice barely above a whisper. "After the way you treated me last week, in front of Sister Atkinson and the other nurses."

Jeremy's jaw clenched, his frustration evident. "My duty is to ensure the welfare of the patients, Grace," he said firmly, cutting her off before she could continue.

But Grace wasn't about to back down. "And is it your duty to look after other nurses in your spare time too?" she challenged, her voice trembling with anger.

Jeremy's expression faltered for a moment, his facade cracking under Grace's pointed accusation. "I don't know what you're talking about," he muttered, avoiding her gaze.

"Really?" Grace shot back, her voice laced with bitterness. " Why are you so bothered about me leaving if you have someone else waiting for you?"

Jeremy's face paled, his features contorted with shock and anger. "That's enough, Grace," he snapped, his voice cold and commanding. "You will stay here and do your duty as a nurse."

With that, Jeremy turned on his heels and stormed off, leaving Grace alone with her thoughts and tears streaming down her cheeks. She couldn't believe what had just happened, the betrayal cutting deeper than any wound she had ever nursed. And as she stood there, grappling with the harsh reality of Jeremy's true feelings, Grace knew that things would never be the same between them again.

Chapter Forty-Two

⁓⁓⁓✦⁓⁓⁓

In the dimly lit hospital room, Grace moved from patient to patient. She walked silently to Percy Hartman's bed. Grace noticed his body still bore the painful marks of the recent fire at the theatre. She looked at him with sorrow in his eyes. How could a hero end up so injured when he had saved so many people from dying?

After her interaction with Jeremy, she wiped her eyes again and took a deep breath. She walked up to Mr Hartman's bed. She had only tended to him a couple of times and yet couldn't shake the feeling of familiarity that washed over her. As she looked down and placed her hand gently on his forehead, Percy opened his eyes. It was the first time Grace had looked into them, but she dismissed the flicker of recognition in his eyes as confusion from his injuries.

Grace worked diligently, her mind preoccupied with thoughts of home. In a moment of carelessness with her mind elsewhere, she accidentally brushed against Percy's burns, causing him to wince in pain.

"Ouch!" Percy exclaimed, drawing her attention.

Flustered, Grace kept apologising " Sorry, sorry! My mind's all over the place today."

Percy tried to reassure her, but his words seemed to fall short. She felt bothered about something, and couldn't seem to shake the feeling.

"Don't worry. You seem a little preoccupied with something. Are you alright?" he asked, with concern in his voice.

Grace hesitated. "I'm sorry, I don't want to worry you with my troubles. You are here to get better, not to listen to my problems."

"Try me, I'm a good listener. And it's not as if I have much else to do here."

Grace looked at the patient for a moment, making a quick decision to tell him more. "I have received a letter from home, informing me of my gravely ill ma."

Percy listened attentively, sympathy evident in his eyes.

"Your ma? What's her name?" Percy inquired, his curiosity piqued.

"Kitty," Grace replied, her thoughts drifting to her beloved ma. Grace noticed a change in Percy's expression, a glimmer of recognition passing through his eyes again.

Summoning his courage, he asked, "Do you have any siblings, Grace?"

Grace nodded, her voice barely above a whisper. "I had a brother, Peter. He disappeared after something happened to us all when I was a lot younger. We haven't seen him since."

Percy's eyes widened with surprise, tears welling up in his eyes. "Alice?" he choked out, his voice trembling. "Is it really you?"

Overwhelmed with emotion, Grace couldn't believe what Percy Hartman had just said. Tears streamed down her cheeks as she reached out to him. "Yes, it's me," she whispered, her voice barely audible.

Unable to contain their emotions any longer, the weight of years of searching and uncertainty finally lifted off their shoulders.

"Oh, Peter!" she sobbed. Grace sat down on the chair beside the bed, clasping her hands together. "But tell me, why did you change your name?"

"I suppose for all the reasons that you changed yours. A fear of your past catching up, a change of identity, not wanting to be found by that dreadful foreman."

Grace blinked slowly and let out a breath, she had finally found him. Something she thought would never happen.

They sat together, lost in a moment of reunion, she felt a sense of peace wash over her. With her brother by her side, she knew she was not alone, and felt a newfound sense of hope and determination.

But as the sun began to set outside the hospital window, reality came crashing back. "I have to go, Percy. Ma needs me," she said, determination in her voice.

"Why are you still here then?"

"Someone is stopping me."

"Who? Why would they do that?"

"He won't let me go, it's like he has a hold over me. But I have no choice. I must make him see sense." Grace turned to walk away, her mind racing with thoughts of how to free herself from the unseen shackles that bound her. "I will explain, but I can't talk now. I will be back later when I've seen the other patients."

As she left her brother's bedside, Grace couldn't help but wonder what life had in store for them next. With the knowledge that she had a loving brother by her side, she was more determined than ever to make it home and tell her ma that she had found Peter.

Chapter Forty-Three

As Grace made her rounds on the hospital ward, her heart felt heavy with the weight of the suffering that surrounded her. The soft glow of the gas lamps cast long shadows along the walls, creating an atmosphere of solemnity and quietude. Patients lay in their beds, their faces contorted with pain, their bodies wracked with illness.

Approaching Percy's bedside, she noticed a figure sitting beside him, her presence both familiar and unfamiliar at the same time. It was Nancy, Percy's wife, her eyes filled with a mixture of concern and anticipation. Grace hesitated, unsure whether she should interrupt their conversation or wait for a more opportune moment.

Grace stood against the next bed, trying her best to concentrate on the patient in front of her whilst listening to her brother's conversation.

"Percy, what's the matter?" Nancy, his wife said.

He looked at the expectant performer sitting beside him, knowing that what he was about to say would change the family dynamics forever. "I have something to tell you, Nancy."

Nancy's heart skipped a beat, the feeling of butterflies fluttered in her stomach. She took a deep breath in and held it for a couple of seconds. "What is it? Should I be concerned?"

"No, no! At least, I don't think so."

"Don't keep me waiting. Has it got anything to do with how close you were with that nurse when I walked in?"

"Sort of, but there's no need to be alarmed."

Grace shifted her head slightly to the side and gasped quietly, she did not know what Percy was about to tell his wife.

Nancy sucked in her cheeks, her mouth pouting, waiting for her husband to give her the news.

"The thing is, I know that nurse," Percy said.

Nancy looked over to follow Percy's gaze. "I was right! When I walked in I thought you were both far too close just to be nurse and patient." Nancy stood up, pushing the chair back, the legs scraping against the wooden floor. Percy winced at the noise, and then the ward fell silent.

"Nancy, sit down, please."

She slowly sat down and pulled the chair a little closer again.

"Remember me saying I haven't seen my sister in years? I suppose I gave up finding her."

"Go on," Nancy said, curiously.

Percy beamed with joy. "She's here, Nancy. Right here in the hospital. I found my sister."

Chapter Forty-Four

Nancy's expression was one of quiet encouragement, inviting Percy to break the silence after his revelation.

Grace, whilst still attending to the patient in the next bed, breathed a sigh of relief. She felt her heart relax and an overwhelming blanket of comfort washed over her as she discovered Percy had accepted her into his life.

"Nancy," he began, "are you pleased?"

Nancy's eyes widened with curiosity, her surprise clear in Percy's earnest tone. She shifted in her chair, her attention wholly on him.

"Yes, of course I am. But, last time you spoke of her, you hadn't seen her since you ran away from home all those years ago."

"I know. I'm as surprised as you are."

"Percy, it's a wonderful—" Nancy's words were interrupted.

Grace took a deep breath and found the courage deep within her to approach her brother. Holding a thermometer, her cheeks tinged with a blush, Grace cleared her throat with a hint of embarrassment.

"I didn't mean to intrude," Grace murmured, her voice gentle and a tad sheepish.

Percy's smile was warm, his concern clear. "No intrusion at all, Grace. Please, allow me to introduce you to Nancy."

As Grace came closer, Percy introduced her to his wife, their gazes locking with a hint of recognition.

"Nancy, this is Grace, my sister," Percy's voice brimmed with warmth. "Grace, my wife, Nancy."

Nancy extended a friendly smile. "I'm confused. Percy said your name was Alice."

"We had to change our names, our lives were in danger in very different ways." Grace bowed her head and gazed towards the floor.

"I understand," Nancy said. "It must have been terrible for you all. Nevertheless, it's a pleasure to meet you, Grace."

"Likewise, Nancy. I've read about you in the papers. Never thought we'd meet, especially like this."

Nancy brushed off the remark. Her fame was now familiar. "Thank you for taking care of Percy. I imagine finding out he's your brother was a surprise."

"It was. I thought I'd never see him again after me and ma fled from the workhouse." Grace's smile held a weight.

Percy looked at his sister and his concern peaked. "What's the matter, Grace?"

"I'm still bothered by Archie's letter. Our ma appears to be sick, and he says she may not pull through."

Nancy frowned. "Then why are you still here? You should go see her."

"Jeremy disagrees," Grace's eyes glistened.

"Who's Jeremy?"

"Grace's beau. He is a doctor here," Percy responded.

"Jeremy should want what's best for you, not just himself," Nancy said.

A blush tinted Grace's cheeks as her gaze dropped.

"Sorry, perhaps that's too much. But trust me. If Jeremy truly loved you, he'd support what's best for you," Nancy said.

Percy nodded in agreement, smiling at his sister.

"Grace, family matters most," Nancy added gently. "Your ma needs you now. Don't let fear or duties stop you from seeing her. You will regret it forever if she dies."

Grace's eyes welled, a mix of gratitude and unease in her gaze.

With a trembling voice, Nancy continued, emotions raw. "I've felt the pain of missed chances, not being there for loved ones. Don't repeat it, Grace. Time with your ma is precious."

Tears streaked Grace's cheeks, her inner turmoil visible. "But what if I lose everything? What if I lose him?"

Nancy's gaze burned, her voice fervent. "Grace, love shouldn't hold you back from where you're needed. You can bridge the gap, but not the lost time with your ma."

Grace's eyes moved from Nancy to Percy, his agreement unspoken but palpable.

Grace wiped tears from her face, determination and sadness intertwining, and asked, "What about Percy? We've only just been reunited." And now there is you too, Nancy. It's like having a second family to consider."

Nancy and Percy exchanged a glance, understanding unspoken.

"Go to her, Grace. Percy and I will still be here when you return. We can get to know each other properly when you have seen your ma, but right now, she is more important than anybody else."

Grace's shoulders dropped, and she sighed with relief. She no longer had the burden of the decision. "You're right. I must go. Thank you for showing me what matters."

Chapter Forty-Five

Grace hurried through the corridors of the hospital, her mind consumed with thoughts of her ma. The weight of Percy and Nancy's words lingered in her mind, urging her to take action before it was too late. Losing her ma without saying goodbye was unbearable for her.

As she rounded a corner, she caught sight of Jeremy standing in the corridor, his expression stern and disapproving. Her heart sank at the sight of him, knowing that he would try to stop her from leaving. But she couldn't let his concerns hold her back any longer. She had to be with her ma during her time of need.

Jeremy reached out to grab her elbow as she passed, but Grace hesitated, her courage shining through. She shook off his grasp, her determination unwavering as she continued on her way. She didn't owe him an explanation, didn't owe him anything at all.

As she stepped outside into the cold, lashing rain, she pulled her shawl tightly around her, trying to shield herself from the biting wind.

The streets were dark and quiet, the last of the costermongers and ragpickers making their way back to their dreary, damp ridden slums. The faint glow of the gas lamps cast eerie shadows along the cobblestones. In the distance, the heavy air held a tangible smog, a reminder of city life's harsh realities.

Her footsteps echoed against the damp street as she hurried along, her heart pounding with a mixture of nervousness and excitement. She worried about seeing her ma, fearing she wouldn't make it in time. But also excited at the prospect of finally being with her during her time of need.

Mixed feelings swirled within her as she thought of Archie, unsure of what their reunion would bring. She had missed him terribly during her time at the hospital, but now she wasn't so sure of her feelings towards him. She couldn't deny the bond they shared, but she also couldn't ignore the doubts that lingered in the back of her mind.

Grace pulled her shawl around her once more and boarded the omnibus.

Chapter Forty-Six

Grace's heart raced with apprehension as the omnibus rattled along the familiar streets of her hometown. She couldn't shake the feeling of unease that gnawed at her insides, uncertainty clouding her thoughts. What would she find when she returned home? How was her mother truly faring? And how would Archie react when she finally saw him again?

Grace stepped down from the horse-drawn omnibus. She looked both ways and breathed in the familiarity of the Whitechapel streets. She started walking towards Nathaniel and her ma's house, steeling herself for the inevitable. And as she reached the front door, with trembling hands, she knocked hard.

"Grace? What are you doing here?"

"Nathaniel! It's so good to see you. How is ma?"

"Is someone there, Nathaniel? I can hear voices."

Grace smiled at her step-father and he stepped to one side with a smile on his face to let her pass.

To her surprise, Kitty was sitting up in a chair by the fireplace, a faint smile playing on her lips as she spotted her daughter. Relief flooded through Grace as she rushed to her ma's side, enveloping her in a tight embrace. "Ma, you're sitting up! How are you feeling?"

Kitty returned the embrace, her eyes shining with warmth. "Much better now that you're here, my dear," she replied, her voice tinged with gratitude. "But how did you know I was ill?" Kitty looked from Nathaniel to Archie, then back at her daughter.

Grace glanced over at Archie, who was fidgeting nervously in the corner. His cheeks flushed with embarrassment as he spoke up. "I—I was worried about you, Kitty. I thought Grace had a right to know," he admitted sheepishly.

A wave of realisation washed over Kitty as she realised what had happened whilst she was sick in bed. Her suspicions evaporated, replaced by a sense of gratitude for Archie's honesty. "Thank you, Archie," she murmured, giving him a grateful smile.

With the tension lifted, Kitty and Nathaniel filled Grace in on everything that had happened during her absence. They shared tales of everyday life, of challenges and triumphs, of moments both joyful and bittersweet.

"I still can't believe you were so sick, ma. I thought—I thought you were—"

"None of that, Grace, your ma is on the mend and feeling much better, aren't you, Kitty?"

"I am. It was melancholy Grace. I was worried about losing my husband again, you weren't here, and I felt glum. I couldn't wake some days. I wanted to hide away from everything and felt anxious." Kitty thumped her fists on the arms of the chair. "I still feel angry at the thought of Nathaniel being taken away even though he was doing good for our benefit."

"Don't worry, ma, we are all back together now."

"Yes, but for how long, Grace?"

Grace had been kneeling at the side of her ma's chair. She stood up wearily, the weight of the worry obvious on her slender frame.

Nathaniel cheerily changed the subject. "Why don't I make Grace a cup of tea, she must be thirsty after her journey."

"And ravenous!" Grace shouted after her step-father.

When they were all back together in the living room, Grace listened to what had been happening in the lives whilst she had been working at St. Thomas. One mind on what her family were saying, and the other in the distance, worrying about Jeremy catching up with her.

As Grace listened to their stories, she felt a sense of belonging wash over her. This was her family, her home, and no matter what trials they faced, they would face them together.

She fell into the warmth of her family's embrace, a sense of comfort enveloped her. It felt as though she had never left, as though time had stood still in their home. Yet, beneath the surface of tranquillity, a storm raged within her, a storm of uncertainty and fear that threatened to consume her.

As Kitty, Nathaniel, and Archie regaled her with tales of their daily lives, Grace couldn't shake the nagging worry that lingered in the back of her mind. She longed to confide in them, to share the burden that weighed heavily on her heart, but the words caught in her throat, suffocated by fear and shame.

Instead, she buried her troubles beneath a facade of smiles and laughter, pretending that everything was fine, that she was fine. But inside, she felt like she was drowning, suffocating beneath the weight of her own silence.

As the evening wore on and the fire burned low, Kitty and Nathaniel broached the subject of Grace's future. "You know, dear, I've been thinking whilst you've been sitting here," Kitty began, her voice gentle but firm. "You should return to St. Thomas' as soon as you can. It's obvious you are missing it, you've hardly said two words all evening. I expect your mind is elsewhere on the wards, not here with us."

Grace's heart skipped a beat at the mention of St. Thomas'. The thought of returning to the hospital filled her with a sense of dread, a reminder of the trials she had faced and the secrets she had kept hidden.

Nathaniel nodded in agreement, his expression serious. "You have a gift, Grace," he said, his voice brimming with pride. "You're meant to be a nurse, and we won't stand in your way."

But Grace hesitated, her mind swirling with doubt and uncertainty. How could she return to St. Thomas' when Jeremy's shadow loomed over her, a constant reminder of the pain and humiliation he had inflicted upon her?

"I don't know, ma," she stammered, her voice faltering. "I'm not sure I'm ready to go back."

Kitty and Nathaniel exchanged a concerned glance, sensing Grace's hesitation. "Is something troubling you, dear?" Kitty asked gently, her brow furrowed with worry.

Grace opened her mouth to speak and finally unburden herself of the secrets she had been carrying, but the words caught in her throat, as she was suffocated by fear and shame once again. How could she tell them about Jeremy and admit that she wasn't as strong as they believed her to be?

"I'm just nervous, I suppose," she replied, her voice barely above a whisper. "But I'll think about it, I promise."

Kitty and Nathaniel exchanged a concerned glance, but before they could press her further, Grace rose from her seat, the weight of her secrets pressing down upon her like a leaden cloak. "I think I'll turn in for the night," she said hastily, her voice strained. "I'm tired."

As she made her way to her room, Grace couldn't shake the feeling of guilt that gnawed at her insides. She knew she should confide in her ma and Nathaniel, tell them about Jeremy and the torment he had put her through, but the words remained trapped inside her.

And so, as she lay in bed, staring up at the ceiling, Grace made a silent vow to herself. She would find the courage to speak her truth, to unburden herself of the secrets that weighed heavily on her heart.

Meanwhile, Archie watched as the one and only woman he had ever wanted take herself to bed and, he vowed to find out what was troubling her.

Chapter Forty-Seven

⁕

Nathaniel found Grace sitting in the kitchen, her hands wrapped around a cup of tea. "What is it, Grace? You know you can tell me. You haven't been right since you stepped through the door last night, no matter how much you tried to hide it with the joy of seeing your ma."

Grace hesitated. "Please don't tell ma, she will worry. It would be a shame if she was ill again after recovering from her dark thoughts."

Nathaniel reached across the table to take hold of his step-daughter's hand. "It's a doctor at work. I thought he loved me. He was so nice when I met him and I hoped we had a future together, but things changed so quickly."

Nathaniel smiled and nodded a little, encouraging her to continue.

"He criticised where I lived, he shouted at me for doing the wrong thing with a patient when I thought I was saving his life. And the ultimate betrayal was when—when I saw him with someone else." Grace shed a tear and wiped it away with the cuff of her nightgown.

"Oh, Grace, that's terrible."

"I couldn't believe it, Nathaniel. I was so humiliated. Everything he said to me made me question my worth in his eyes. And after seeing him with someone else, it was like I meant nothing to him. He has shattered my heart."

"Were you going to marry him?"

"I thought I would at first, but now I don't want to go anywhere near him. It's going to be hard because I work with him, but I must be strong and concentrate on the patients."

"Please don't see him again. He is a dangerous and despicable character and doesn't deserve you. I know it's hard wanting something better for your life, and you will do anything to get it, but he's not worth it. I'm sorry, Grace, but I won't ever give my permission for you to marry him. A gentleman asking for your hand in marriage falls to me now, and I want to honour what your pa would want for you and it's not him."

"I know. In fact, I've had serious thoughts about him whilst I've been here. He did not make it easy for me coming home to see ma. He was abusive and made me feel guilty for wanting to come home, so I'm not sure why I would want to spend my future with him."

"Do you think there will be trouble when you return?"

Grace shrugged her shoulders. "No, I don't think so. He will be too involved in other women to notice I'm even there. I deserve better."

Nathaniel smiled at his step-daughter. "I think Archie is wanting to speak to you."

"I know. I just don't know what to say."

"You don't have to say anything, wait for him to speak first. I know he still likes you, he has been willing to wait, and to me, that is the sign of true love."

Grace stood up and walked over to Nathaniel. She opened her arms and they hugged tightly. "I love you so much Nathaniel for everything you have done for us, I don't think I could ever repay you."

"Go and finish your studies, that's how you can repay me."

There was a gentle knock at the door and it creaked open slowly. "Grace?" Archie said.

Chapter Forty-Eight

After a few moments of uncomfortable silence, Nathaniel smiled at both Archie and Grace, then left the room.

They called each other's name.

"Archie—"

"Grace—"

"Please, Grace, you go first."

"Oh Archie, I didn't know how much I would miss you. I tried so hard to fall in love with someone else, to deny that I was in love with you, but I couldn't. I only said no before I left because I didn't want us to hold each other back if we both met someone else."

"I know," Archie said, reaching for her hand. "I sensed that after what you had said. But then, when you wrote to me and told me all about Jeremy, I thought you might have been in love with him and got married. Your courting seemed serious."

Grace sighed. "I thought it was, but I'm so glad it didn't turn out that way, it wasn't meant to be. I don't want to be with someone like that."

"Like who? He didn't hurt you did he?"

"No, well not physically anyway."

"What do you mean?"

"Just emotionally. He made me feel that I was beneath him when I first started courting him, then he said I was a good nurse, then he was abusive when I said I needed to leave to see my ma."

"Sounds like a dodgy character to me, I don't like the sound of him."

"Well, he's out of my life romantically now. I don't want someone like that, but what it did show me is how much I missed you."

Archie hesitated before placing his arm around Grace's shoulder. "I know, and I missed you too. It still stands, you know."

"What does?"

"What I said before you left. I still want to marry you Grace, I want children with you and have a family that we both love and adore." He reached and wiped a tear away from under Grace's eye. "I hope they are tears of happiness, Grace."

"Oh, Archie, of course they are. But there is just one problem."

"What? Not more obstacles, surely?"

"No, Archie. It's just that I really do want to finish my studies. I must complete what I set out to do."

"I would encourage that, Grace. I would never stop you."

"Isn't that wonderful!" Nathaniel came bounding into the room without notice.

"Pa! Were you listening in?"

"Erm, not intentionally, I just—"

Archie and Grace both looked at each other and laughed.

"Don't worry, pa, we don't mind, do we, Grace?"

"No, not at all. It's good that you are here to share our news."

"And of course, Grace, I would be delighted to give permission for you both to marry," said Nathaniel smiling. "Come on, we must tell your ma. She will be thrilled to hear your news."

Archie led Grace upstairs by the hand ready to tell Kitty the news he had been wanting to announce for what felt like years.

"This is wonderful, both of you. I had secretly hoped this would happen one day."

"Thank you, ma. Oh, and I almost forgot! How could I?" Grace jumped up from the side of her ma's bed with a spring in her step.

"Don't look so buoyant without telling us what's going on, Grace. What is it?" Kitty said, reaching for her daughter's hand.

"I've found him, ma."

"Found him? Found who?"

"It's Peter, I found Peter."

Kitty looked at her daughter, then brought a hand to her mouth and cried tears of happiness. "My son, my beautiful son," she exclaimed, before grabbing hold of her daughter and hugging her tightly.

Epilogue

As Kitty stood before her son, Peter, her heart threatened to burst with a torrent of emotions. Years of longing, guilt, and torment seemed to culminate in this single moment. She studied his face, every line and contour familiar yet so different from the last time she saw him. Guilt gnawed at her insides, a relentless reminder of the choices she made and the pain she caused. Yet, as Peter enveloped her in a warm embrace, she felt a glimmer of hope amidst the turmoil of her emotions.

"Peter," she whispered, her voice barely audible as tears welled up in her eyes. "I've missed you so much, my boy."

Peter held her tightly, his embrace offering a sense of comfort and forgiveness she never thought she'd experience. "I've missed you too, ma," he replied, his voice choked with emotion.

"I'm so, so terribly sorry for leaving you. I didn't know what to do. I was terrified, and Grace was right by my side. I had no choice but to run away."

"I know, ma, I don't blame you. I felt lost at first, I wondered if you were ever coming back, but I knew it was for the best. I just wish I had known you were both safe."

"Peter," she reached across to take his hand.

"It's Percy, ma. I'm not sure if Grace told you, but I felt I had no choice but to change my name. I wanted a fresh start with the Morgans who took me in. They chose it."

"You have a new family?"

"Don't look glum, ma. They could never replace what I had with you, pa, and Grace. But I needed help, they took good care of me. They fed me, loved me, and gave me hope."

Kitty let out a long, drawn out breath, releasing the anguish and torment that had built up over the years. She felt relieved she was now reunited with her boy. "I'm pleased for you, Peter, I really am."

"Percy, ma. It's Percy."

"Oh, I know," she laughed. "But to me you will always be Peter. I will get used to it in my own good time."

Percy didn't want to push it, he knew she had been through a tirade of heartache and finding her son would have been both overwhelming but welcomed.

They stood there for a moment, lost in their shared embrace, the weight of the years of separation melting away. For Kitty, it felt like a lifetime of burden had been lifted from her shoulders, replaced by a sense of peace she hadn't known in years.

After a few moments of silence, Kitty turned to Percy. "Did Grace tell you I re-married?"

"Briefly, ma. Are you happy?"

"Incredibly. Don't get me wrong, I miss your pa terribly. I wrestled and toyed with my emotions for a long time. I questioned whether it was the right thing to do. But to be honest I couldn't have survived without Nathaniel. I think you will like him."

"If you chose him, ma, I'm sure I will."

"He saved me and your sister from poverty. He took us in when he didn't have to. He was a shining light in the darkness and days of gloom and grief."

"I'm pleased for you ma, please don't be hesitant in telling me what happened. I feel like I need to know everything that's happened, so I feel close to you and Grace again."

"We will talk over time, I'm sure of it. And tell me about your family? Nancy seems a good woman for you, having met her briefly at the theatre."

"She is wonderful, ma, as is Lilly. I don't know what I would do without them." Percy smiled at the fondness of his family. "Would you like to meet them properly?"

"Of course I would," she said, looking around.

Percy stood up from his chair and placed his hand on Kitty's shoulder, giving her a sign that everything would be okay. "Nancy, come through my love, bring Lilly."

Kitty found herself drawn to Percy's wife, Nancy, and their young daughter, Lilly. Tears of joy filled her eyes as she looked upon her granddaughter for the first time, a beautiful reminder of the love and hope that persisted despite the trials they had faced.

"She is more beautiful than I remember, Percy."

"Thanks, Kitty, I think Lilly is beautiful too," Nancy said, adding a touch of humour to the sensitive and heavy atmosphere in the room.

Everyone laughed and cooed over Lilly, who was now crawling along the floor.

Kitty couldn't help but feel overwhelmed with gratitude for the family she had gained, a second chance at happiness she never thought possible. "It's lovely to meet you both properly," she said, her voice trembling with emotion.

As they settled into conversation, sharing stories and laughter, Kitty couldn't shake the feeling of overwhelming joy that filled her heart. Here, surrounded by her son and his family, she felt a sense of belonging she hadn't known since the days before everything fell apart.

But as the conversation turned to Grace, Kitty felt a surge of excitement building within her. "There's something I have to tell you, Percy," she said, a mischievous twinkle in her eye.

Percy looked at her, curiosity piqued. "What is it, ma?"

A smile spread across Kitty's face as she revealed Grace's surprise announcement. "Grace is marrying Archie," she said, excitement bubbling in her voice.

"Archie? Thank goodness for that! She finally said no to Jeremy did she? I never liked the man."

"You met him?"

"He looked after me in the hospital after the fire. Good at his job, but not worthy of my sister."

"That's good to know, I'm delighted that she and Archie are getting married. It seems to have taken them a while to get to that decision, but all in good time."

As they basked in the glow of their shared happiness, Kitty couldn't help but feel a sense of gratitude for the journey that brought them to this moment. Despite the trials and tribulations they faced, their love for one another had endured, stronger than ever.

And as they looked towards the future, united in love and forgiveness, Kitty knew that no matter what challenges lay ahead, they would face them together as a family.

As the evening drew on, the family shared a meal together, laughter and conversation filling the air. Kitty marvelled at the life her son had built for himself, grateful for the kindness and love he had found with Nancy and Lilly.

As they sat around the table, Kitty couldn't help but feel a pang of sadness at the thought of the years she had missed, the moments she would never get back. But as she looked around at her family, the love and warmth in their eyes filled her heart with hope for the future.

As the evening came to a close, Percy turned to his mother with a smile. "Ma, it's been a long time since we've been together and, I hope you'll come and visit us again very soon," he said, his voice filled with sincerity.

Kitty nodded, her eyes shining with tears of happiness. "Of course, my dear," she replied, her voice filled with emotion. "Try to keep me away."

And as they bid each other goodnight, Kitty felt a sense of peace settle over her, a newfound sense of belonging she hadn't known in years. As she drifted off to sleep that night, surrounded by the love of her family, she knew that no matter what the future held, they would face it together, as a family united in love, happiness, and forgiveness.

About the author

If you haven't yet read the second book in the series, ***The Starlet Slum Girl***, you can download it here: https://mybook.to/TheStarletSlumGirl

My free book, ***The Whitechapel Angel***, is also available for download here: https://dl.bookfunnel.com/xs5p4d0oog

About the Author:

I have always been passionate about historical romance set in the Victorian era. I love to place myself on the dark, murky streets of London and wonder what it would have been like to overcome tragedy and poverty to find true love. The different classes of society intrigue me and I'm fascinated to know if love ever truly prevailed between the working and upper class.

I'm not sure about you, but whenever I visit the streets of Whitechapel, or read historical books from the bygone era, I find myself transported back to a time when I once lived there myself. Some say past lives are a myth, past life transgression is a 'load of tosh,' and you only ever live this life in the now. But whether you believe in past lives or not, for me, I easily feel myself living in those times.

With each book, I strive to create stories that capture the heart and imagination of my readers, bringing to life the strong, resilient characters that live in that bygone era.

When not writing, I can be found exploring the great outdoors with my husband Mike, and my Jack Russell, Daisy, or curled up with a good book. There is nothing quite like lighting the log burner and a candle or two, and turning the pages.

Stay connected:

Please, if you have any feedback, email me at anneliesemmckay@gmail.com (my admin assistant,) and I will respond to all of you personally.

Printed in Great Britain
by Amazon